PREFACE

With the introduction of NEP -2020, there is going to be a paradigm transformation of School Education as well as Higher Education. Gone are the days when cramming the learning material and academic vomiting in the examination hall was the rule of the game to score good grades. Innovative Teaching-Learning Processes, both on-line and off-line, with Learner-centric delivery and Objective assessment of learners; Outcome Based Education; Application Oriented teaching; Program outcomes focused learning will inculcate the required skill sets and problem- solving capabilities among the learners.

We were thrilled to learn about the transformations in education system intended to be made phase-wise in future over a period of time. We salute the NEP team-members, who came out with this excellent document intending to incorporate many innovative practices in the education system, required so desperately. Having many decades of experience in education sector, and training over one thousand faculty members in last twenty-five years, we have learnt the art of explaining them the contents in a learning-centric mode.

The pandemic gave us an opportunity to deliver many on-line programs explaining NEP-2020 provisions to different faculty/students of Schools and HEIs, and it also motivated us to write this book. The book, having 8 chapters, explains various aspects of NEP-2020 in brief, and the Opportunities & Challenges encountered by the School Teachers and HEI faculty in the process of implementation of the policy. Some Possible Solutions are also indicated therein.

The book is dedicated to our numerous students, peers and faculty members, who made us to offer, time and again, innovative explanation to many fundamental concepts, thus helping us to learn better.

Dr. Avadhesh K. Khare
khareavadhesh@gmail.com **9950221111**
Dr. H. K. Sahjwani
harisahjwani@gmail.com **9871679878**

ABOUT AUTHORS

PROF A. K. KHARE:

Email ID khareavadhesh@gmail.com

Mobile: 9950221111

Born in 1946, Prof. A. K. Khare acquired B.E.(Hons.) in 1966, M.Tech. in 1973, Ph.D. 1985 in Mechanical Engineering from GEC Jabalpur and IIT Kanpur.

He has served as:

- Director/ Professor, Institute of Engineering & Technology, Lucknow,
- Pro-Vice Chancellor U.P. Technical University Lucknow,
- Vice- Chancellor, IEC University, Baddi (H.P.),
- (Hon.) Chancellor, IEC University, Baddi (H.P.),
- CEO, Pratap University, Jaipur (Raj.)
- Vice- Chancellor, Suresh Gyan Vihar University, Jaipur (Raj.)
- Chairman Central Admission Board of U.P. State Engineering Admission Test Cell & Conducted Common Entrance Examination in the State of U.P. for 10 years.
- Chief Project Coordinator for UP state in "World Bank Program" TEQIP of Govt. of India.

- Conducted FIRST On-Line entrance examination in the Country ENAT as Controller of Examinations in 2007 & 2008.
- Chairman/ Member of over 30 committees of Govt. of India/ UGC/ UP State Govt on issues like Planning, Coordination, Policy formulation and Development activities in Technical Education, Accreditation, Curriculum Development, Faculty Development, Entrance Examination & Counseling,
- Advisor, Technical Education Dept., Govt. of U.P for 2 years
- Chief Advisor Sharda Group of Institutions, Sharda University Gr Noida for 3 years
- Guided 25 candidates in M Tech/ Ph D thesis; Published over 100 research papers
- Career of over 57 years in planning, development, admissions, counseling, quality assurance, regulation & facilitation in technical education.

Current interests include Design & Conduction of FDPs, Conducting programs on **NEP 2020** for Schools & University faculty.

Presently associated with Quantum University, Roorkee (Uttarakhand) as [Hon.] Advisor.

PROF. H. K. SAHJWANI

Born in September 1944

Academic Journey:

Lecturer in Physics at S.D. College Panipat for 18 years.

Head of Physics Department for 15 years.

National Level Contribution:

Member of the Board of Studies (Physics) at K.U.K.

Innovator and Researcher:

Developed cutting-edge physics courses.

Pioneered Nano-technology syllabus development.

Published numerous research papers in esteemed national journals.

Spearheaded innovative experiments in Physics using Arduino.

Administrative Excellence:

Head of Applied Science Department and Dean Academics at IEC College of Engineering Technology.

Planned infrastructure for Applied Science and B. Tech courses.

Contributed to the growth of APIIT S D India, affiliated with Staffordshire University, U.K.

Author and Educator:

Authored textbooks for classes XI and XII.

Conducted influential workshops and conference presentations.

Awards and Recognitions:

Received "Man of the Year Award" from the American Biographical Institute Inc.

Life member of the Indian Association of Physics Teachers and the Indian Society for Technical Education (ISTE).

Technological Innovator:

Developed operational software for sugar mills, exporters, accounting, and physics experiments.

Proficient in multiple programming languages and application software, including Arduino programming.

Visionary Leader:

Fostered academic and administrative excellence.

Introduced mentorship programs and guided faculty members.

Nurtured countless students, resulting in numerous awards in various competitions.

Email: harisahjwani@gmail.com
Mobile: 9871679878

SALIENT FEATURES OF THE BOOK

- Briefly ***Overviewing*** NEP-2020, and the paradigm transformation of School Level & HEIs Level Education system, to promote *Skilling, Make -in India, Creativity, & Education Quality* in general.
- Discussing the ***Opportunities and Advantages*** available in NEP-2020 to the students, teachers, Institutions and other stake-holders to improve the Education Quality.
- Carried out in-depth discussions with the concerned persons [teachers, students].
- Identifying ***Challenges, Difficulties,*** the Students, Teachers, Institutions may face in implementation of the Policy.
- Suggesting ***Possible Solutions,*** wherever possible, to meet the Challenges.

Dr. Avadhesh K. Khare
Dr. Hari K. Sahjwani

PUBLISHER: Notion Publisher

ISBN NUMBR:

NEP-2020 - OPPORTUNITIES & CHALLENGES

CHAPTER-1 SYSTEM OF HIGHER EDUCATION

1.1 INTRODUCTION: OVERVIEW OF NEP-2020

TRANSFORMATION OF EDUCATION SYSTEM:

In NEP-2020 there is a clear shift of the basic conceptual definition of education from "Education as transmission of expert knowledge" to "***Education as building learning competencies including learning to learn and life- long learning"*.**

The ***FOCUS*** of the education system is unambiguously identified as:

- Students learn how to learn i.e. self-learning,
- How to think critically and solve real time problems,
- How to be creative and multidisciplinary,
- How to innovate, adapt, and absorb new material,
- Pedagogy must evolve to make education more experiential, holistic, integrated, inquiry-driven, discovery-oriented, learner-centric, discussion-based, flexible, and, enjoyable,

- Teacher Training, Refresher Programs, Continuous Professional Development are embedded in Policy document.

1.2 The Identified Action Points Are:

- Recognizing, identifying, fostering the ***unique*** capabilities of each student.
- **Flexibility**; No hard separations on Stream Basis e.g.: Science, Arts, Commerce, Law, Engineering, Medical etc.
- Multi-disciplinarity, Holistic education.
- Emphasis on conceptual understanding, Creativity and critical thinking.
- **Ethics, Human & Constitutional values**: empathy, respect for others, cleanliness, courtesy, democratic spirit, spirit of service, respect for public property, scientific temper, liberty, responsibility, equality, and justice.
- **Life skills**: communication, cooperation, teamwork, and resilience, respect for diversity and local context.
- Full equity and inclusion.
- Synergy in curriculum across all levels.
- Outstanding Research to enhance learning outcomes across the country.
- Multiple Entry/ Exit Options for students to pursue the program at their choice.
- ***Extensive*** use of technology.
- Focus on regular formative assessment.

1.3 New School Education

- The children in the age group 3 to 8 years learn very fast in curiosity-based, play-based and enquiry-based mode.
- Three valuable years of early stage of growth of

the children i.e. 3 to 6 years, are not effectively utilized in schools for structured learning.

- They informally learn in their homes through their elders, based on the free time available to the elders.
- In the new 5+3+3+4 structure, a strong base of ***Early Childhood Care and Education (ECCE)*** from age 3 is also included, which is new, and is aimed at promoting better overall learning, development, and well-being.
- ***ECCE*** shall be delivered through a significantly strengthened system of institutions consisting of anganwadis ; pre-primary schools; stand-alone pre-schools through teachers, specially trained in the curriculum and pedagogy of ***ECCE***.
- Anganwadi workers/teachers shall be given a 6-month certificate program in competency building. The program will cover early literacy, numeracy, and other relevant aspects of ECCE.
- These programs may be run through digital/distance mode using suitable technology through smartphones, allowing teachers to acquire ***ECCE*** qualifications.
- In the longer term, cadres of professionally qualified educators for early childhood care and education shall be prepared, through stage-specific professional training, mentoring mechanisms.
- The **C**ontinuous **P**rofessional **D**evelopment (**CPD**) of initial professional educators will be ensured.
- The current learning crisis in our country is of very large scale, at all levels.
- Help of willing and competent students may be explored to support teachers in the mission of attaining universal foundational literacy and numeracy.

- The children easily expose their problems/deficiencies before their friends, rather than before their teachers.
- Thus, ***incentive-based peer tutoring*** can be taken up as a voluntary and joyful activity for fellow students under the supervision of trained teachers and by taking due care of safety aspects.
- ***Each- one teach- one*** concept may be followed to handle this large issue, wherein a literate member of the society/ community shall commit to teaching one student/person how to read and write.
- New Innovative models may be established to foster such peer-tutoring and volunteer activities, as well as launch other programs such as each-one teach-one to support learners in this nationwide mission to promote foundational literacy and numeracy.
- It is very significant in any schooling system to ensure that children are enrolled in the school and are also attending school on a regular basis. Unless the majority of them regularly attend the school, the actual learning would not happen.
- Through initiatives such as the ***Samagra Shiksha*** and the ***Right to Education*** *Act*, India has made remarkable strides in recent years in attaining very high enrolment in elementary education.
- The tragedy of the current education system is that it is neither entrepreneurship & job oriented, nor focused on creativity & innovation, even no emphasis is given on life management skills training, which is an essential part of everyone's life.
- NEP will focus more on experiential learning, skill development, knowledge enhancement, games and

sports integrated education, and will develop creative and innovative ability among learners.

- For example, ***vocational training from 6th class***, innovative courses and ***computer coding in middle program*** phase, ***10 days bagless period***, and using ***some days of holidaying to improve knowledge and various skills***, are necessary to change the mindset and developing creative and innovative attitude.

Only one board exams for 10th and 12th class may be conducted. It will ease parents and children from unwarranted pressure causing many health issues and, in few cases, suicidal tendency or actual suicide. Children can focus more on developing other life skills and competitive exam studies.

Local Language

- Teaching in local language also helps a country to grow culturally and economically, since the students naturally learn at a much faster rate.
- Later students learn to use English or any other language as a communication language on a global platform, as and when required.
- Life skill training will help in overall personality development. ***Sanskrit language*** is again given prominence, which is vital culturally, scientifically and developing memory and intellect.

Duration	Age Group		Class	Program
5 Years	3 Years	[3-6years]	Pre-School/Angwadi/Play School	Foundational
	2 Years	[6-8years]	Class 1, 2	
3 Years		[8-11 yrs]	Class 3, 4, 5	Preparatory
3 Years		[11-14 yrs]	Class 6, 7, 8	Middle
4 Years		[14-18 Yrs]	Class 9, 10,11, 12	Secondary

- Many universities across the globe have started teaching Sanskrit owing to its benefits on memory and intellect.
- There are numerous changes and benefits that we are going to see in future, as we progressively implement NEP provisions at school level and at higher education level in years ahead.
- This change won't take place in a day or two. However, it will be implemented gradually in the coming months/years and hopefully will be implemented totally ***by 2035 or 2040***.
- The learners needed to be nurtured from an early age, as 3–8-year age group is the golden period of development of a child. The children need to be attracted towards school, and ***they should love coming to schools*** rather than being forced / dragged to go to school. Early childhood education should be enjoyable and play with fun.
- In the NEP the school education is grouped in four programs.

1.4 School Education (5+3+3+4)

- The curricular framework for school education will therefore be guided by a 5+3+3+4 design, consisting of the Foundational Stage (in two parts, that is, 3 years of Anganwadi/pre-school + 2 years in primary school in Grades 1-2; together both covering ages 3-8), Preparatory Stage (Grades 3-5, covering ages 8-11), Middle Stage (Grades 6-8, covering ages 11-14), and Secondary Stage (Grades 9-12 in two phases, i.e., 9 and 10 in the first and 11 and 12 in the second, covering ages 14-18).
- In all stages, experiential learning will be adopted, including hands-on learning, arts-integrated and

sports-integrated education, story-telling-based pedagogy among others, as standard pedagogy within each subject, and with explorations of relations among different subjects.

- To close the gap in achievement of learning outcomes, classroom transactions will shift towards competency-based learning and education.
- The assessment tools will also be aligned with the learning outcomes, capabilities, and dispositions as specified for each subject of a given class.
- Students will be given increased flexibility and choice of subjects to study, particularly in secondary school, including subjects in physical education, the arts and crafts, and vocational skills, so that they can design their own paths of study and life plans.
- Holistic development and a wide choice of subjects and courses year to year will be the new distinguishing feature of secondary school education.
- There will be **full flexibility** and there will be no hard separation among 'curricular', 'extracurricular', or 'co-curricular', or among 'arts', 'humanities', and 'sciences', or between 'vocational' or 'academic' streams. Subjects such as physical education, the arts and crafts, and vocational skills, in addition to science, humanities, and mathematics, will be incorporated throughout the school curriculum, with a consideration for what is interesting and safe at each age.
- States may look into innovative methods to achieve these aims of greater flexibility and exposure to and enjoyment of a wider range of subjects, including across the arts, sciences, humanities, languages, sports, and vocational subjects.

- In addition to high quality offerings in Indian languages and English, foreign languages, such as Korean, Japanese, Thai, French, German, Spanish, Portuguese, and Russian, will also be offered at the secondary level to enrich their global knowledge and mobility according to their own interests and aspirations.

FOUNDATION PROGRAM

- The FOUNDATION Program is to inculcate eagerness among children to rush to School from the comfort of home.
- There will be ***no examination*** in this part of program.
- The fun, art, music, dance, drama, and puppetry can all be incorporated in the games that include drawing, painting, and other visual arts.
- ***ECCE*** will provide play-based, activity-based, inquiry-based learning that is flexible, multifaceted, and multilevel to enhance the child's overall development.
- The focus will be on alphabets, numbers, counting, colours, shapes, sounds, words, collaborations within the class, puzzles requiring logical and critical thinking, developing sensitivity, good behaviour, courtesy and ethics, personal and public hygiene, and cooperation between the student and the teacher.
- Six-month certificate/ one-year diploma programs in ECCE for teachers may be offered to educate them to handle 4–5-year child who has more questions than you have answers.
- This program has a basic program outcome PO which inculcates eagerness among the children to rush to school. Child eagerly wants to come to school to

play with friends; and the child is not forced / dragged to go to School.

- Once, a child and his father were going along a road. There was another man on the road, who was pulling the animal with the help of the rope. The child saw them and asked his father, *whether the animal is being pulled and dragged to take admission in any school?*

Preparatory Program

- The PREPARATORY program will be delivered in local / regional / national language and optionally in English (may be by some schools).
- The young minds will be introduced to examination in this phase and the pedagogy will be based on the play, discovery, and inquiry / activity-based learning.
- The program outcome PO of this phase of the program is that children continue to have fun and play with friends; learn very simple things as alphabets, numbers, counting etc; focus on their motivation in attending school.

Middle Program

- In the MIDDLE program Computer/Coding and may be some basics of AI will be introduced along with one Indian Language.
- Focus will be on Vocational Education such as: Carpentry, Smithy; Plumbing; Cooking; Sewing; Home Science; First Aid; Health Care; Electric work, Metal work, Gardening, Pottery making etc.
- The main PO of this phase of the program will be that the students acquire proficiency in some vocational skills to be able to earn livelihood, should the circumstances so demand.

Secondary Program

- The 4-year SECONDARY program may have semester system with no fixed stream-oriented curriculum.
- The controlled and guided flexibility will be available in opting subjects under the guidance of faculty/student mentor, including physical education, the arts and crafts, hobby courses, vocational and technical skilling courses, in order to empower learner.
- The focus of education in this phase will be on critical thinking with no cramming.
- One foreign language such as German, French, Russian, Spanish will be introduced in this program.
- All subject matter content will be simplified to its essentials, so students are able to learn in regional language / Indian language using inquiry-based, discovery-based, group discussion-based, and analysis-based learning approaches.
- The program outcome PO of this phase will focus on choice-based flexibility in opting the courses; no cramming; project-based and inquiry-based learning; introducing self-learning.

Examination & Assessment

- The Examination & Assessment System for student-development will undergo total transformation.
- The focus at present lies on the end semester examination, which is conducted only once in the duration of the course, and poor performance in the examination in general cannot be easily rectified.

- The method of cramming the subject contents, and pasting it in the answer book, thereafter, will be done away with, and not be practiced.
- Instead of the present method, the examination will be 360^0 based on assessment by various stakeholders.
- It will be based on ***learning outcomes*** of the courses/topics at the learning level / Blooms level as prescribed in the curriculum.
- The students will be trained to accept examination as one of the components of learning.
- Their sufferings from examination phobia will be drastically reduced.
- The Assessment System will include (i) self-assessment by the learner (ii) peer assessment by the classmates (iii) progress of the child in project-based and inquiry-based learning, quizzes, roleplays, group work, portfolios, etc., (iv) teacher assessment.
- The weightage of these components of assessment may not be equal and depend on many factors.
- The application – based questions will be designed to assess the depth of understanding by the learner.
- Some sample questions at different levels are given below only for the sake of explaining the examination and assessment philosophy and do not reflect the actual questions from any specific area of study.

1.5 SAMPLE QUESTIONS

Preparatory Level

Q 1: Two men were walking together. Somebody asked them, "How are you related?". One of them replied, "*Iski Bua meri Bua ko Bua kahti hai.*" How are they related?

Middle Level

Q 2: What is the number "?"

[7 + 8] =? [Easy]

[2 +?] x 5 = 30 [Moderate]

[2 +(3+?)] x 5 = smallest *3- digit* perfect square. [Innovative]

Q 3: A man, a tiger, a goat & a bundle of grass have to cross a river using a boat, which can accommodate any two at a time. At any point of time tiger & goat; and goat & grass cannot be left alone together for obvious reasons. How to cross the river in the least attempts?

Q 4: Few birds are sitting on two trees. A bird from tree-1 says to bird of tree-2 " If 10 birds fly from your tree to my tree, we shall be equal in numbers." The bird from tree-2 replies, " If 10 birds fly from your tree to my tree, my number will be 5 times your number." How many birds are there in each tree?

Secondary Level

Q 5: A top spinning about its vertical axis is slightly displaced making the axis inclined. Then, the top starts revolving about the vertical axis in the direction …

(a) Counter-clockwise CCW

(b) Clockwise. CW

(c) Any direction: CCW or CW

(d) Depends on the direction of spin of the top.

Q 6: A man weights 600 N, lifts a load P N, while standing on the Weighing machine. What is the value

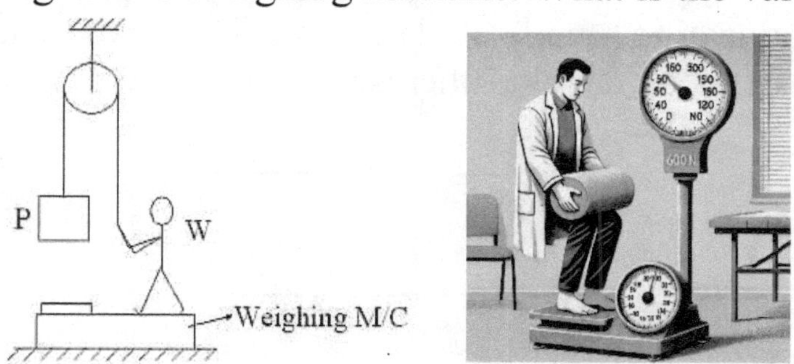

of P if the reading of the weighing machine is 150N.

Q 7: The earth spins on its axis in CCW direction and revolves around the Sun also in CCW direction. Imagine that both motions go CW. Then:

A says that "the pattern of sunrise & sunset will change". B says that "the pattern of Time zone will change". C says that "the weather pattern of seasons will be reversed". Who is/are right?

Q 8: A faulty balance beam ACB, 30 cm long, has fulcrum C 14.5 cm from the left end A. Some person weighs wheat, by putting 10 Kg weight on the left pan A, and wheat on the right pan B. Then, he puts the 10 Kg weight on the right pan B, and wheat on the left pan A. If the beam is shown perfectly balanced each time while weighing, what is the actual total weight of the wheat?

Q 9: A pulley D, carrying load P, can slide along a 5 m long cable ADB, whose ends A & B are attached to walls, 4 m apart. At what height 'h' should B be located above A, so that the tension T in the cable is minimum.

Changes in higher studies must be aligned with industry, business or professional requirement in engineering, medical, law, etc. This will help our students to develop themselves as job creators, will

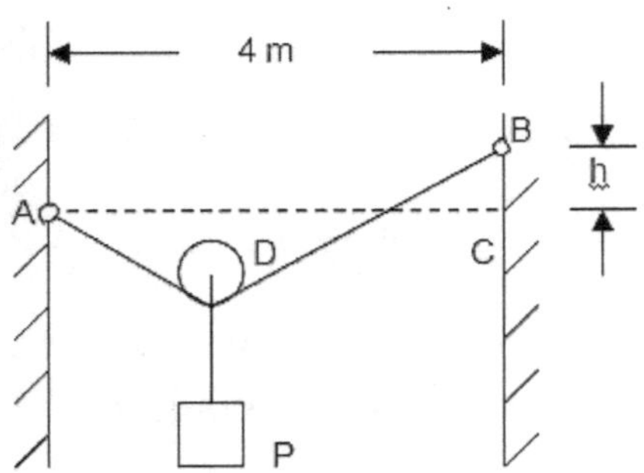

help them in seeking job easily, will generate huge numbers of innovators and creators to attract global investors and consumers. Budget is likely to be enhanced 3.5 folds on education to develop schools, colleges to international level, and to match the prevailing market needs and overall development of a child. It will help to create "*India a Global Knowledge Superpower*".

The Union Education Minister, on 28thJuly 2023, reiterated the commitment of the Government to ensure phase-wise implementation of NEP 2020 in totality in the country within the prescribed time period, and discussed the steps taken in last three years.

NATURE OF HEIs:

There shall be only FOUR types of HEIs, based on their Vision/Mission in the country in due course of time.

- **Research-intensive Universities**: those that place equal emphasis on teaching and research.

- **Teaching-intensive Universities**: those that place greater emphasis on teaching but still conduct significant research.
- **Autonomous degree-granting College (AC)**: Multidisciplinary institution of higher learning that grants undergraduate degrees.
- **MERUs** (**M**ultidisciplinary **E**ducation and **R**esearch **U**niversities) at par with IITs, IIMs.
- **Affiliating Colleges** may be granted ***AC*** status; **or** try to get converted into a university; **or** become Constituent college of any university. The affiliating college status shall cease to exist.
- Constituent college would be fully a part of and owned by the university.
- Deemed to be university, affiliating university, affiliating technical university, unitary university shall be replaced simply by 'University' on fulfilling the criteria as per norms.
- Single-stream HEIs will plan to become multidisciplinary, else will be phased out by 2035.
- Multidisciplinary universities and ACs, (with at least one in or near every district), and with more HEIs across India that offer medium of instruction or programs in Local/Indian languages.

1.6 REGULATION & GOVERNANCE:

SINGLE WINDOW REGULATION

- The Higher Education Commission of India **(HECI)**, the sole regulating body will be established, with Four different functions of regulation being handled by four independent verticals within this umbrella institution.
- National Higher Education Regulatory Council **(NHERC)** will function as the common, single point regulator for the higher education sector.
- **N**ational **A**ccreditation **C**ouncil **(NAC)** will be responsible for Accreditation of institutions and Quality Assurance, which will award graded accreditation to institutions, largely based on the learning outcomes and effective utilization of resources, & quality assurance.
- The **H**igher **E**ducation **G**rants **C**ouncil **(HEGC)** will carry out funding and financial assistance to higher education sector, disbursing scholarships and developmental funds for launching new focus areas and expanding quality program.
- The **G**eneral **E**ducation **C**ouncil **(GEC)** will frame expected learning outcomes for different higher education programs, also called 'graduate attributes'. Higher education qualifications leading to a degree/diploma/certificate shall be described in terms of learning outcomes. Professional Councils such as, ICAR, VCI, NCTE, CoA, NCVET etc. will act as professional standard setting bodies as members of GEC.
- All education institutions, private and public, will be treated at par with similar standards of audit and disclosure.

- The effective governance and leadership that enables the creation of a culture of excellence and innovation will be ensured.

BOARD OF GOVERNORS

- A **B**oard **O**f **G**overnors (BOG) of the institution shall be established consisting of a group of highly qualified, competent, and dedicated individuals having proven capabilities and a strong sense of commitment to the institution.
- The BOG will be empowered to govern the institution free of any external interference , including that of Government.
- New members of the Board shall be identified by an expert committee appointed by the Board itself.
- Equity considerations will also be taken care of while selecting the members.
- All leadership positions and Heads of institutions will be offered to persons with high academic qualifications and demonstrated administrative and leadership capabilities along with abilities to manage complex situations.
- The impartial, merit-based, and competency-based selection shall be carried out by the BOG through a process led by an **E**minent **E**xpert **C**ommittee (**EEC**) constituted by the BOG.
- While stability of tenure is important to ensure the development of a suitable culture, at the same time, leadership succession will be planned with care to ensure that good practices that define an institution's processes do not end due to a change in leadership. Leadership changes will come with sufficient overlaps, and not remain vacant, in order to ensure smooth transitions.

- Excellent faculty with high academic and service credentials, demonstrated leadership and management skills will be identified early and trained through a ladder of leadership positions by BOG.
- Each institution will make a strategic Institutional Development Plan approved by the BOG, on the basis of which institutions will develop initiatives, assess their own progress, and reach the goals set therein, which could then become the basis for further public funding.
- The IDP shall be prepared with the joint participation of Board members, institutional leaders, faculty, students, and staff.

1.7 OPPORTUNITIES:

The Government of India will have to take several steps/actions for facilitating the smooth implementation of NEP by providing guidelines/directions/support.

1. The ECCE is a strategic decision in the policy to nurture the children from a very early age, when their leaning competency is at its peak.
2. Teaching in local language/ regional language even at higher classes will certainly enhance the learning competency of the children.

3. Introducing computer coding, introduction to AI, Vocational and Skilling courses and One International Language at middle and secondary level will make the learners job-ready and prepare them for need based advance courses.
4. Making selection of courses fully flexible in the program, provides the students ample chances to pursue his hobby/passion/choice-based courses.
5. There will be full flexibility in choosing the courses in a program of study, and there will be no hard separation among 'curricular', 'extracurricular', or 'co-curricular', or among 'arts', 'humanities', and 'sciences', or between 'vocational' or 'academic' streams.
6. Holistic development and a wide choice of subjects and courses year to year will be the new distinguishing feature of secondary school education.
7. Multiple Exit/Entry options will empower the student to complete the program at his convenience.
8. Stigma of "**FAIL**" will be done away with "**NOT YET PASSED**" making life of the students tension-free.
9. The Single-Stream affiliated institutions are provided ample opportunities to become multi-disciplinary degree awarding Autonomous Institutions over a period of time.
10. Presently, they have to look at the Affiliating University for many aspects.

- Autonomy is academic freedom with responsibility.
- University curriculum changes are too slow.

- In autonomous institutes, changes can be at a pace of one's choice depending on industry and societal requirements.
- It can provide better employability of graduates.
- Proud feeling and ownership about institute.
- Autonomy leads to excellence.
- New outcome-based accreditation can be easily achieved through effective use of autonomy.
- Clear Vision, Mission, Goals, Strategic planning.
- Measuring attainment of program outcomes.
- Teaching learning process and Learning evaluation, Continuous improvement.
- The BOG of the Institutions has been given sufficient power to run and govern the institutions without any external interference.
- An **E**minent **E**xpert **C**ommittee (**EEC**) constituted by the BOG will select persons for all leadership positions and Heads of institutions in an impartial, merit-based, and competency-based selection without any external interference.
- Outstanding leaders will be identified and developed early, working their way through a ladder of leadership positions.

1.8 Challenges:

- NEP has made provisions to transform the entire education system gradually over a period of time, which was so much needed for a long time.
- But the implementation of the provisions has to be well thought of and gradual, so that transition indigestion does not result while implementing.
- All the stakeholders, such as promoters, management, administration, faculty, students, employers, industry have to be educated properly so

that the understanding of NEP provisions is proper, accurate, adequate, and acceptable.

- Else, they will result into challenges and hurdles in future.
- High-quality ECCE across the country could be a major challenge because of the volume of the task involved.
- Help of willing and competent students, and other suitable methods maybe explored to support teachers in the mission of attaining universal foundational literacy and numeracy.
- Each-one-teach-one is one such innovative concept identified, but its implementation at such a large scale across the country causes concern. This task has to be properly implemented in a phased manner.
- Sanskrit language is again given due prominence in a big way. Although necessary, a large number of Sanskrit scholars will be required to handle the issue.
- The option of exiting after Grade 10 requires that the education at this level should be partially complete. Should the student want to discontinue further studies for financial/social reasons or otherwise, the program outcomes of Grade 10 education should provide some livelihood/job to the student,.
- The increased flexibility and choice of multiple subjects even at school level may result into a very large number of diverse groups of students having different combinations of subjects. The institutions, educators, teachers have to be ready to face the situation.

- States may have to search into innovative methods to achieve these aims of greater flexibility and exposure to the students.
- During the schooling period while learning in his local language, if the child is migrated to some other state having different language of instructions, how the child will continue his studies?
- Will there be a uniform admission-criteria countrywide for all the schools in different states, or will they have their own choices?
- In the event of mid-term migration, there could be a variation in vocational courses/skilling courses/hobby courses available at some other location in the school where he is seeking admission.
- If due to mid-term migration there is no institution at new place which has same subjects as subjects taken by students before migration then what will the student do?
- Some kind of general uniformity in the availability of courses at different locations have to be ensured for the sake of continuity.
- How can we compare the similar grades / marks / percentiles awarded by different schools / States / Examination boards? Do we have to moderate them using some equivalence formula.
- Will BOG appoint, promote, reward the faculty, employees, director, VC without ***Govt interference at any level, whatsoever?***
- The very existence of single stream affiliated HEI seems to be at stake. Can they still survive, or **Single Stream-HEI** will become extinct and if so, in what period?

- Can **Single Stream-HEI** become a constituent college of some University by retaining the ownership of the institution by the promotors?
- Can **Single Stream-HEI** themselves decide their fee, programs, admissions, international students, etc. and for how long.
- What is the difference between UGC and HECI. Will UGC / other regulators constituted through ACT of parliament will continue to exist, and with what level of regulating authority?
- Like in the western world, do we plan to Grade Our Universities at Global level?

1.9 Possible Solutions to Challenges

- To address creation of trained man-power suitable for ECCE, where children in the age group 3-6 years have to be handled, it is suggested that preference should be given to women, who are naturally empowered to handle the kids. Suitable feedback-oriented, incentive-based schemes may be created for awarding the compensation. Such women can be given additional training in the pedagogical aspects of ECCE.

- In the event of mid-term migration, the child may complete the current session at the old place, and then shift to new place.
- Like the provisions in Central Schools, the migrated students should be given priority in merit-based choice of their schools across the country.
- Large, budgeted investment in ECCE must be made, which has the potential to give all young children such access, enabling them to participate and flourish in the educational system throughout their lives.
- The provisions of quality early childhood development, care, and education must be achieved as soon as possible, say within 6-8 years, to ensure that all students entering Grade 1 are school ready.
- The Government of India has identified that "A **N**ational **C**urricular and **P**edagogical **F**ramework for **E**arly **C**hildhood **C**are and **E**ducation **(NCPFECCE)** for children up to the age of 8 will be developed by NCERT.
- The Key Goal will be to ensure universal access to high-quality ECCE across the country in a phased manner. Special attention and priority will be Key Goal socio-economically disadvantaged. ECCE shall be delivered through a significantly expanded and strengthened system of early-childhood education institutions."
- State Governments shall prepare cadres of professionally qualified educators for early childhood care and education, through stage-specific professional training, mentoring mechanisms, and

career mapping. Necessary facilities will also be created for the initial professionals.

- **C**ontinuous **P**rofessional **D**evelopment ***(CPD)*** of ECCE educators should be taken up at war footing.
- "Highest priority of the education system will be to achieve universal foundational literacy and numeracy in primary school by 2025. National Mission on Foundational Literacy and Numeracy." This concept is built-in the policy document and shall help in the resolution of Challenges.
- The exit option after Grade 10 necessitates that the Program Outcomes PO of school education up to class 10 and PO up to class 12 must be tubular in nature.
- The program outcomes of Grade 10 education should contain ***enough skilling / vocational courses*** to provide some livelihood/ job to the student, should the student want to discontinue further studies for financial/social reasons or otherwise after class 10.
- A pool of retired educators/teachers/persons, who have served education for about 25-30 years and are willing, knowledgeable and energetic, may be created at the state level, give them the required training/tips, and assign them specific task of explaining and educating the stakeholders (on-line or off- line mode) about the advantages of provisions of NEP.
- They may serve as ***Knowledge Experts*** (may be given a token honorarium) to spread the light of knowledge to the needy groups, society and community in many issues including the following.
- The flexibility and choice of multiple subject combinations at school level may result into a very large number of diverse groups of students having different subject groups.

• Further, they will have different hobby/passion/skilling/vocation courses of their choice.

• The institutions, educators, teachers have to be ready in advance to face the problem of time-table preparation for [students, teachers and classrooms]; creating common group for some course out of multiple combinations of courses. The ***Knowledge Experts*** may help in this matter.

• The flexibility and choice of making useful combinations of essential and optional courses best suited for the program the student is intending to pursue, will be a big task to address and explain to students seeking admission in higher education programs. The ***Knowledge Experts*** may help in this matter.

• The multiple entry/exit options, available to the students in UG,PG programs may result into several combinations of options available to the students, causing enough confusion needed to be clarified. The ***Knowledge Experts*** may help in this matter.

• MHRD should prepare a webpage for school students indicating the multiple options available to the students who want to discontinue the studies after schooling.

• The students should be advised therein the choices of essential courses needed while schooling to avail these options. The ***Knowledge Experts*** may help in this matter.

• In the event of mid-term migration of students, the issue of matching local/regional language, matching the available courses of studies etc. may be addressed by some expert committee assisted by some ***Knowledge Experts.***

- The Single-Stream affiliated institutions are provided ample opportunities to become multi-disciplinary degree awarding Autonomous Institutions. The ***Knowledge Experts*** may help in this matter.

Chapter-2 Programs & Curriculum

2.1 FLEXIBILITY, MULTIPLE ENTRY/EXIT OPTIONS

Generic Objectives of Education:

• Transmission of old knowledge; creation of new knowledge,

• The development of wisdom in the use of knowledge for purposeful application.

• To inculcate curiosity within students to accept challenges of new problems in life.

• To earn livelihood and sustaining a family in future.

• To serve the society, industry, community and country.

• To be a good human being, respect for values and ethics.

Process of Learning:

The process of learning consists of following steps.

• **Motivation:** The curiosity and eagerness in the learner to learn.

• **Apprehension:** The perception of the learning material/source.

- **Acquisition:** The co-relation of information/ knowledge to what he already knows.
- **Retention:** The process of storing the information.
- **Recall:** Retrieval of information when necessary.
- **Generalization:** Developing strategies to process information for new situations.
- **Performance:** Putting strategies into practice; Application of knowledge/ information.
- **Feedback:** Feedback permits him to update knowledge from his previous performance.

Learning Objectives:

Some of the Learning Objectives are indicated below.

- **Reading:** A low-level objective. Enables the student to read the text.
- **Understanding:** Be able to understand the meaning of what he reads.
- **Retention:** Retains the information.
- **Assimilation:** Understands what is not written. Can read/interpret between the lines.
- **Recall:** Retrieves the relevant information when needed.
- **Reasoning:** Can reason out logically in a sequential manner on the topic he has learnt.
- **Analysis:** Analyses the information. Learns why it is so?
- **Ideation:** Learns the process of generating Ideas. New examples. New applications. Analogy.
- **Simulation:** Imagination. Can simulate the meaning/ applications/ solution in his mind's eyes.
- **Application/ Self- Learning:** Application of knowledge/ information in new situation to which he

was not exposed to earlier. Problem solving capability. Self-learning.

Teaching- Learning Techniques:

Some of the activities the teachers can do by themselves to improve learning include, but are not limited to, the following.

- Flexibility in assessment creates interest towards the topic.
- Interest creates curiosity, that leads to ideation and innovations.
- Try to improve your current presentation in preparation, content and delivery.
- Yourself award marks out of 10 to your current lecture after delivering it.
- Note down good questions that the students asked in the class.
- Note, what you yourself have learned from the discussions in the class during the delivery of lecture,
- Anticipate provocative questions/queries in respect to your lecture you are going to deliver.
- Do not be too quick to help the student, who is struggling to *frame the answer*.

- You must interest yourself in the *student* as much as the *subject material*.
- The teaching-learning techniques include the following.
- **Expository**- Expose students to new knowledge/ information. They learn from observation. Expose, and then explain.
- **Explanatory-** Explain the concept to student and make them understand.
- Provide **alternate explanation** if he is not understanding.
- **Guided Discovery-** This is student -centric approach; Let the student observe & reason out. Observation & Logical reasoning often leads student to discover new knowledge. This is time consuming but very effective.
- **Experiential Type-** Direct or simulated experience; use of support facilities- video & multimedia; industrial visits; labs. Observing during industrial visits followed by explanation; Doing experiments in labs., Video shows.
- **Exploratory-** Students learn through exploration. Self-Learning. Transfer & application of knowledge. Major projects; New situations; Unconventional Design problems; Using internet & Google.
- **Deny a Fact** - Negate a fact. Student learns to argue to justify his point. Develops logical reasoning capability.

Flexible Academic Systems

- The rigid system of learning offers negligible flexibility to students in selecting the courses of their choice and helps little in becoming a well-rounded personality.

- As part of providing quality education and making the graduates employable and industry ready, the NEP has provided Flexible Credit Based System (FCS) in all academic programs.
- Various surveys (governmental, as well as non-governmental), indicate that we are currently in a learning crisis.
- Curriculum content will be reduced in each subject to its core essentials, to make space for critical thinking and more holistic, inquiry-based, discovery-based, discussion-based, and analysis- based learning.
- The mandated content will focus on key concepts, ideas, applications, and problem- solving capabilities.
- Teaching and learning will be conducted in a more interactive manner; questions while learning will be encouraged, and classroom sessions will regularly contain more fun, creative, collaborative, and exploratory activities for students providing deeper and more experiential learning.
- Students will be given increased flexibility, and choice of subjects to study, particularly in secondary school, including subjects in physical education, the arts and crafts, and vocational skills, so that they can design their own paths of study and life plans.
- The system is flexible enough to permit the students to credits instead of marks, which are credited/deposited to his account in Academic Bank of Credit.
- Thus, the students can opt courses of their choice and alter the pace of learning within the broad framework of academic course and credit requirements of the program.

- FCS allows students to draw their own academic plan depending on their capability and choice and alter it as they progress in the program.
- Students are given freedom learn at their own pace: Slow pace; Normal pace; or Fast pace and complete the program after earning the required credits.
- The Credit is defined uniformly for all programs by UGC; as C = L + T + 0.5 P, where L T P have conventional meaning.
- A semester will have 13 to 15 working weeks. Thus,13 to15 hours of Lecture and Tutorial or 26 to 30 hours of Practical/ Field work in a semester constitutes One Credit.
- Total average credits per semester may range from 18 to 20.

Curriculum

- The curriculum of any course consists of the [i]the course syllabus, [ii] the learning objectives, [iii] the delivery mechanism of the course content, [iv] the assessment of learning outcomes; all taken together.
- Curricular Integration of Essential Subjects, Skills, Vocational/ Technical Skills, Value & Ethics, Hobby, Sports, Passion Courses will be reflected in curriculum.

• The curriculum of a Program will contain courses grouped under various heads, viz. **1. Program Core**

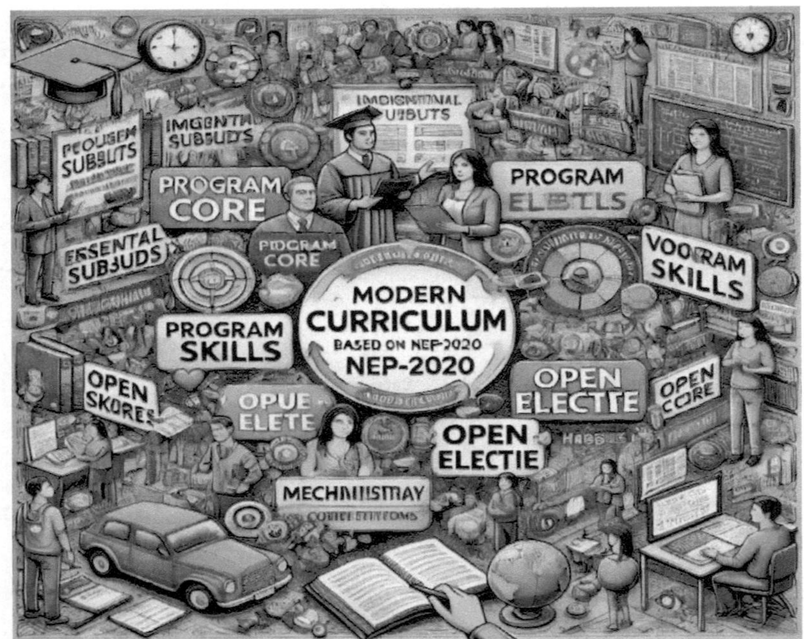

(PC), Major 2. Program Elective (PE), Minors 3. Open Core (OC), Value & Ethics, Environment, Sustainability, Equity and **4.Open Elective (OE),**Vocational; Skilling, Sports, Hobby, Passion, Music + **Delivery** + **Assessment of Learning Objectives** in the course.

• An Academic Counsellor/Personal Tutor will help the student in selecting the courses based on program requirement, course prerequisites, student's ability and interest in various academic disciplines.

• Imaginative and flexible curricular structures will enable ***creative combinations*** of disciplines for study and would offer multiple entry and exit points.

• Students will enjoy the flexibility to move from one discipline/program of study to another.

- Ample options are available to choose interdisciplinary courses from other Schools, which will help the student to develop additional skills. Faculty/expert/peer guidance will be available to the students in this exercise.

The ***new curriculum framework*** prepared by the government in accordance with provisions of NEP-2020, will have several features regarding guided flexibility given below:

- Opportunity for learners to choose the courses of their interest in different disciplines.
- Facilitating multiple entry and exit options with UG certificate/ UG diploma/ or UG degree, depending upon the ***program objectives*** and credits earned.
- Flexibility for learners to move from one institution to another to enable them to enjoy multi and/or interdisciplinary learning and earning credits from the very best of the institutions to be credited in ***Academic Bank of Credit*** account.
- Flexibility to switch to alternative modes of learning (offline, ODL, and Online learning, and hybrid modes of learning).
- Semester may comprise of 90 working days, with summer term may be for eight weeks. About 50% of total program credits should be earned through core courses in the major discipline.

2.2 LOCAL/REGIONAL/NATIONAL LANGUAGE

• Sanskrit, possesses a classical literature that is

greater in volume than that of Latin and Greek put together, containing vast treasures of mathematics, philosophy, grammar, music, politics, medicine, architecture, metallurgy, drama, poetry, storytelling, and more written by people from all walks of life, religion and a wide range of socio-economic backgrounds over thousands of years.

• Sanskrit will thus be offered at all levels of school and higher education as an important, enriching option for students, including as an option in the three-language formula. It will be taught in ways that are interesting and experiential as well as contemporarily relevant, and in particular through phonetics and pronunciation.

• Sanskrit textbooks at the foundational and middle school level may be written in Simple Standard Sanskrit (SSS) to teach Sanskrit through Sanskrit (STS) and make its study truly enjoyable.

• Delivery of educational content in Local / Regional

/ National Language.

- English will be optional, like any other foreign language.
- The NEP 2020 emphasizes the importance of multilingualism in education, advocating for the use of local, regional, and national languages as mediums of instruction to enhance cognitive development and cultural understanding.

2.3 MODULAR 4 YEAR UG PROGRAM

- Multiple entry/exit options will be available like in a train [one can board the train on any station and get off mid-way. Then, again take another train on the same route. He has not to repeat the journey performed.].
- The students have not to repeat the courses in which they have earned the credits in any program, if they leave the program mid-way.
- After completing a certain number of credits, students can exit the program with a recognized qualification (Certificate after 1 year, Diploma after 2 years, bachelor's degree after 3 years, and a bachelor's degree with research after 4 years).
- Students have the opportunity to re-enter the program to complete their education and earn higher qualifications at their convenience.
- The programs will be modular in nature, permitting smooth multiple exit/entry options.
- Mid-way exit may be associated with the award of some certificate/ diploma/ degree respecting the relevant credits earned by the student during the academic journey.
- Discontinuing the program mid-way shall not be

the total loss of credits earned and education achieved.

- Program Objectives of these certificate/ diploma/ degree programs must be tubular/linear in nature to facilitate multiple exit/entry.
- Imaginative and flexible curricular structures will enable creative combinations of disciplines for study and would offer multiple entry and exit points.
- 'Liberal Arts' will be brought back to Indian education.
- Institutions and faculty will have the autonomy to innovate on matters of curriculum, pedagogy, and assessment.
- Empowering the faculty to conduct innovative teaching and research will be a key motivator and enabler for them to do truly outstanding, creative work.
- Excellence will be further incentivized through appropriate rewards, promotions, recognitions, and movement into institutional leadership.
- Department of Language, Literature, Music, Philosophy, Indology, Art, Dance, theatre, Education, Mathematics, Statics, Pure and Applied Sciences, Sociology, Economics, Sports, Translation and Interpretation, etc. may be established in Indian universities.
- Inclusion of research and internships in the undergraduate curriculum.
- Professional or General education will aim to organically evolve into institutions/clusters offering both seamlessly, and in an integrated manner by 2030.
- Artificial Intelligence (AI), 3-D machining, big data analysis, and machine learning, in addition to genomic studies, biotechnology, nanotechnology,

neuroscience, with important applications to health, environment, and sustainable living that will be woven into undergraduate education for enhancing the employability of the youth.

2.4 ACADEMIC BANK OF CREDIT [ABC]

We can change our mobile phone service provider [from AIRTEL to JIO to VODAPHONE and vice-versa] retaining the SAME mobile number due to advancement and availability of suitable technology. Similarly, if we transfer our bank account from one branch to another, the account number remains the same.

- A centralized **Academic Bank of Credit** will be constituted at Govt. of India level, where every student at all Schools/Autonomous colleges/ Universities pan India will be required to open their Academic Account, which will be fixed and unique for every student and linked with his Aadhar card.
- Academic Account, which will be fixed and unique for every student and linked with his Aadhar card. Thus, every student will have his unique academic account number (linked to Aadhar Card), which remains the same irrespective of changing Institution / University / Program, and all the academic Credits earned by him at any time will be credited/deposited to his personal academic account for all times to come.
- These academic entries in his account are permanent and cannot be manipulated/ moderated/ edited/ changed in future by anyone, including himself, for any reason, whatsoever.

- The academic account of any student will reflect complete record of Credits earned/ Degrees obtained/

Institutions studied/ all academic matters.

- Credits earned from any University relevant to the program shall be credited in the personal account of the student in *the National Level Academic Bank of Credit*.
- He can study different courses in the other University of his choice and deposit the credits earned in ABC personal account.
- He can start earning credits and decide the *PROGRAM* mid-way of the studies in the program.

- He is also permitted to change the program of study mid-way but has to earn the credits required in the new program.
- Students can accumulate and transfer credits from different accredited institutions.
- Flexibility available to complete degree requirements by combining credits from various courses and institutions.
- Encouraging lifelong learning by allowing individuals to return to education at any stage of their life to update their knowledge and skills.
- The introduction of an Academic Bank of Credit (ABC) is a significant innovation in NEP 2020, facilitating seamless mobility and recognition of credits earned across institutions.
- Credits acquired in foreign universities will be permitted.

2.5 OPPORTUNITIES

The NEP focuses on:

- Emphasis on the all-round development of students, fostering critical thinking, creativity, and emotional intelligence.
- Aligning education standards with global norms to make Indian students competitive on the international stage.
- Encouraging innovation and research through flexible and interdisciplinary programs.
- Making education accessible to all sections of society, promoting equity and inclusion.
- Students can opt the courses according to their interest and academic ability in completing them.
- The Flexible System allows students in deciding

their academic plan and permits students to alter it as they progress during the program.

- The students will be provided limited guided choices of [the selection of courses/of time/of altering the course plan] depending on his academic ability.
- The Academic Counsellor/ Personal Mentor/ Faculty Mentor will help the student in identifying the courses based on Program requirement, Course prerequisites, Student's ability and interest in various academic disciplines.
- Nurturing & rewarding student's innovative capabilities will be in-built in the system.
- The part credits earned, will be honoured by awarding suitable certificate/diploma, and will not be wasted.
- The curriculum will instil in them Vocational/ Technical Skills, Human values, Ethics and Respect for all the cultures through suitable courses.

2.6 CHALLENGES

- Substantial investment in the education sector in developing the required human-resource and infrastructure is needed to support new initiatives and changed program structures.
- The adequate teacher training, and development in very large numbers is needed to adopt new pedagogical methods and multilingual instructions requiring major investments.
- Coordinating efforts across various states and institutions to maintain synergy, consistency and quality needs massive administrative coordination.
- The traditional educational institutions and stakeholders may offer resistance/hindrance in implementing the changes. This has to be very

carefully handled.

- Securing adequate funding and resources in the budget of all the states for the implementation of new policies and programs is essential.
- Establishing robust mechanisms for quality assurance and accreditation across diverse educational institutions pan India will be the need of the hour.
- Addressing the digital divide to ensure equitable access to technology-enhanced learning the entire education system.
- Effective execution of policies at the grassroots level, ensuring that the intended benefits reach all students.

2.7 Possible Solutions to Challenges

- The state/ central governments should allocate sufficient funds and resources to implement get to demonstrate their intent of implementing the innovative changes suggested by NEP-20.

• A pool of retired educators/teachers/persons, who have served education for about 25-30 years and are willing, knowledgeable, and energetic, may be created at the state level, give them the required training/tips, and assign them specific task of explaining and educating the stakeholders (on-line or off- line mode) about the advantages of provisions of NEP. They may serve as ***Knowledge Experts*** (may be given a token honorarium) to spread the light of knowledge to the needy groups, society and community in many issues.

• The multiple entry/exit options, available to the students in UG, PG programs may result in to several combinations of options available to the students, causing enough confusion needed to be clarified. The ***Knowledge Experts*** may help in this matter.

• The ***Knowledge Experts*** can also serve as Expert Counsellors to discuss with the students in identifying the courses based on Program requirement, Course prerequisites, Student's ability and interest in various academic disciplines.

• Flexible Academic system with multiple entry/exit options and innovative combinations of the courses, make a suitable choice very confusing and difficult for the students. The ***Knowledge Experts*** may help in this matter.

• Creation of several program structures of tubular programs having linear program objectives is a difficult task requiring expertise in development of program structures. The ***Knowledge Experts*** may help in this matter.

• Flexibility to switch to alternative modes of learning (offline, ODL, and Online learning, and hybrid modes of learning) will require establishment of equivalence between them.

- Integration of ***Essential Subjects, Skills, Vocational/ Technical Skills, Value & Ethics, Hobby, Sports, Passion Courses*** will be reflected in curriculum in different proportions in various programs. Imaginative and flexible curricular structures will enable ***creative combinations*** of disciplines for study and would offer multiple entry and exit points. This must be carefully understood by the policy makers and curriculum designers. The ***Knowledge Experts*** may help in this matter.

CHAPTER-3 Unconventional Learning

[Vocational, Skilling, Hobby, Adult, Online, ODL courses]

3.1 Vocational and Adult Education:

- Vocational education and training (VET) play a critical role in equipping students with practical skills that are directly applicable in the workforce. The NEP-2020 emphasizes the integration of vocational education at all levels of education, starting from Grade 6.
- The aim is to ensure that by 2030, at least 50% of learners in the school and higher education system will have exposure to vocational education.
- NEP-2020 envisions the creation of a robust framework for adult education, including the use of technology and innovative teaching methods to reach out to adult learners.
- **Integration in School Curriculum:** NEP 2020 proposes integrating vocational education into

mainstream education from the early stages. This integration aims to expose students to various trades and crafts, allowing them to make informed decisions about their career paths.

- **Skill Development Centres:** The establishment of dedicated skill development centres in partnership with industries and vocational training institutes will provide hands-on training and real-world experience.
- **Industry Collaboration:** Collaboration with industries ensures that the vocational courses remain relevant and updated with the latest technological advancements and market demands.

3.2 Adult Education:

- Adult education focuses on providing lifelong learning opportunities for individuals who may not have had access to or completed formal education during their youth. This includes literacy programs, basic education, skill development, and vocational training.
- **Lifelong Learning Opportunities:** NEP 2020 promotes lifelong learning, recognizing that adults may need to upgrade their skills or acquire new ones to adapt to changing job markets.
- **Flexible Learning Formats:** Adult education programs will be designed to accommodate the schedules of working adults, with options for part-time, evening, and weekend classes.
- **Community-Based Learning:** Community learning centres will be established to provide accessible education opportunities for adults in rural and urban areas, fostering a culture of continuous learning.

3.3 Open Distance Learning and Online Education

The rapid advancement in technology has revolutionized the way education is delivered. Open Distance Learning (ODL) and online education have become essential components of the education system, offering flexibility and accessibility to learners who cannot attend traditional classroom settings. NEP-2020 advocates for the expansion and strengthening of ODL programs, ensuring they are of high quality and aligned with the learning outcomes of traditional programs.

3.4 Open Distance Learning (ODL):

- **Flexibility and Accessibility:** ODL offers flexibility in terms of time and location, making it accessible to learners who cannot attend traditional classes due to geographical, financial, or personal constraints.
- **Use of Technology:** Leveraging technology to deliver educational content, conduct assessments, and provide support services ensures that ODL can be as effective as conventional education.
- **Accreditation and Quality Assurance:** Ensuring that ODL programs meet high standards of quality and accreditation, will enhance their credibility and

acceptance among employers and educational institutions.

3.5 Online Education:

- Online education is blended with experiential and activity-based learning. Pilot studies for online education need to be conducted. Online teaching platform and tools will have to be developed. Online

assessment and examinations, training and incentives for teachers are numerous challenges to conducting online conduction & examinations at large scale, including limitations on the types of questions that can be asked in an online environment, handling network and power disruptions, and preventing unethical practices.

- **Digital Infrastructure:** Investment in digital infrastructure, including high-speed internet and affordable devices, is essential to make online education accessible to all students. Virtual Labs: DIKSHA, SWAYAM, and SWAYAMPRABHA are some examples.

- **Interactive Learning Platforms:** Developing interactive and user-friendly online learning platforms will enhance student engagement and improve learning outcomes.
- **Blended Learning Models:** Combining online education with traditional classroom experiences (blended learning) can offer the best of both worlds, providing flexibility while maintaining a level of personal interaction need to be carefully evolved.

3.6 Hobby and Skilling Courses

Hobby and skilling courses are designed to cultivate students' interests and talents beyond the conventional academic curriculum. These courses encourage creativity, innovation, and practical skills, enabling students to explore and develop their passions. NEP-2020 proposes the introduction of hobby courses in areas such as music, dance, arts, crafts, and sports, as well as skilling courses in fields like coding, carpentry, and home science.The students can pursue their interests and develop skills that are both enjoyable and potentially career-enhancing. This holistic approach to education aims to create well-rounded individuals who are prepared for diverse career paths and personal growth.

- *Vocational Education* [from school level onwards] will make the child employable at early stage.
- ***Skilling, including hobby*** courses must be a part of every program.
- **Integration** of vocational education programs into mainstream education in all education institutions in a phased manner.
- **B.Voc.** degrees introduced in 2013 will continue to exist.
- National Committee for the Integration of Vocational Education (NCIVE) will guide in this matter.
- Adult Education Centres (**AECs**) could also be included within other public institutions such as **HEIs,** vocational training centres, based on the quality of facilities available.
- Adult education courses may include (a) foundational literacy and numeracy; (b) critical life skills (including financial literacy, digital literacy, commercial skills, health care and awareness, childcare and education, and family welfare); application- oriented courses useful to adult age group. May also include (c) vocational skills development (with a view towards obtaining local employment); (d) basic education (including preparatory, middle, and secondary stage equivalency); (e) continuing education (including engaging holistic adult education courses in arts,

sciences, technology, culture, sports, and recreation, as well as other topics of interest or use to local learners, such as more advanced material on critical life skills).

- **Creative Arts:** Courses in music, dance, painting, photography, and other creative arts allow students to explore their passions and develop their talents.
- **Sports and Physical Activities:** Sports and physical education courses promote health, teamwork, and discipline, contributing to the holistic development of students.
- **Extracurricular Activities:** Encouraging participation in extracurricular activities through structured hobby courses can lead to the development of well-rounded individuals with diverse skill sets.
- **Short-Term Certification Programs:** Short-term certification programs in areas such as computer programming, graphic design, digital marketing, and more provide learners with valuable skills that can enhance their employability.
- **Entrepreneurship Training:** Courses in entrepreneurship equip students with the knowledge and skills needed to start and manage their own businesses, fostering a culture of innovation and self-reliance.
- **Technical Skills:** Technical and vocational skills training in fields such as plumbing, carpentry, automotive repair, and electrical work can lead to stable and rewarding careers.

3.7 BRIDGING SKILL GAPS:

- Vocational and skilling courses can address the skill gaps in the workforce, making students job-ready and enhancing their employability.

- Lifelong Learning: Adult education programs provide opportunities for continuous learning and skill development, promoting personal and professional growth.

Flexibility and Accessibility: ODL and online education offer flexible learning options for individuals who cannot attend traditional classes, making education more accessible.

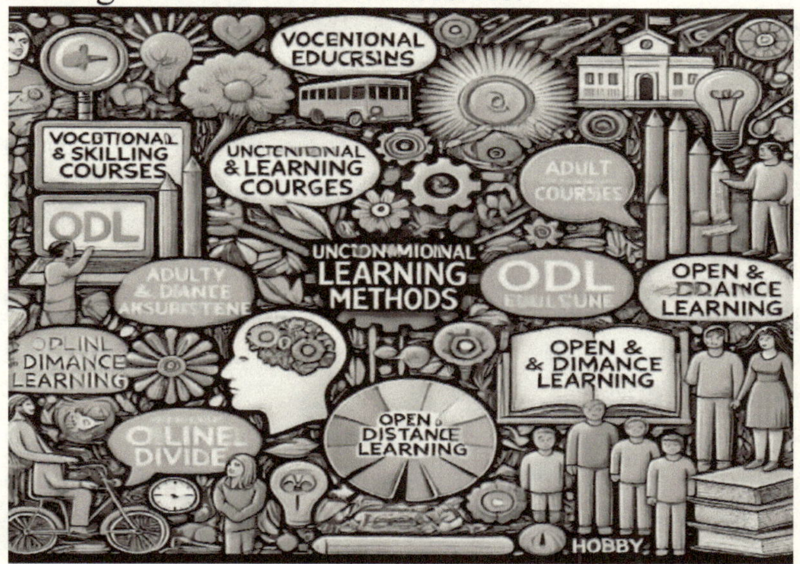

- Holistic Development: Hobby and skilling courses contribute to the holistic development of students, fostering creativity, innovation, and practical skills.

3.8 Opportunities:

NEP 2020 presents numerous opportunities for transforming the educational landscape in India through unconventional learning methods.

- Enhanced Employability: Vocational and skilling courses align education with industry needs, enhancing the employability of graduates.
- Increased Accessibility: ODL and online

education make learning accessible to a broader population, including those in remote areas.

- Holistic Development: Hobby and extracurricular courses contribute to the overall development of students, fostering creativity, physical fitness, and emotional well-being.
- Lifelong Learning: Adult education programs encourage lifelong learning, allowing individuals to continuously upgrade their skills and knowledge.

3.9 Challenges:

- Infrastructure and Resources: Developing the necessary infrastructure and resources for vocational training, ODL, and online education can be costly and time-consuming.
- Teacher Training: Educators need specialized training to effectively deliver vocational, adult, and online education, as well as to manage hobby and skilling courses.
- Learner Engagement: Keeping learners motivated and engaged in non-traditional education settings can be challenging, especially for adult learners and those in remote areas.
- Digital Divide: Ensuring that all students have access to the necessary digital infrastructure is a major challenge, particularly in rural and underserved areas.
- Quality Assurance: Maintaining high standards of quality and accreditation for ODL and online education programs is essential to their credibility and effectiveness.
- Funding and Resources: Securing adequate funding and resources for the development and implementation of vocational and skilling courses can be challenging.

- Cultural Acceptance: Overcoming cultural biases and resistance towards unconventional learning methods, especially vocational education, is crucial for their widespread acceptance.

3.10 Possible Solutions:

To overcome these challenges, the following solutions can be considered:

- **Quality Frameworks**: Establishing robust quality assurance frameworks for vocational, ODL, and online education to ensure they meet national and international standards. Establish clear standards and accreditation processes for ODL and online education programs to ensure they meet high-quality benchmarks. Implement regular monitoring and evaluation of programs to maintain consistent quality and address any issues promptly.
- **Professional Development**: Providing continuous professional development and training for educators to equip them with the skills needed to deliver high-quality vocational, adult, and online education. Provide continuous training and professional development for educators and administrators to maintain high standards in teaching and program management.
- **Innovative Teaching Methods**: Utilizing innovative teaching methods and technology to enhance learner engagement and motivation in non-traditional education settings.
- **Investment in Infrastructure**: Allocating sufficient funds to develop the necessary infrastructure and resources for unconventional learning methods.

- **Partnerships**: Collaborating with industry partners, NGOs, and international organizations to support and enhance vocational training, adult education, and ODL programs.

3.11 Overcoming Cultural Acceptance:

- Awareness Campaigns: Launch awareness campaigns to highlight the value and benefits of vocational education and unconventional learning methods, targeting students, parents, and communities.
- Success Stories: Share success stories of individuals who have benefited from vocational, skilling, and hobby courses to inspire and motivate others.
- Policy Advocacy: Advocate for policies that promote and support unconventional learning, emphasizing its role in the holistic development of individuals and the economy.

3.12 Addressing Resistance to Change:

- Stakeholder Engagement: Engage with all

stakeholders, including educators, parents, students, and industry representatives, to gather input, address concerns, and build consensus on the benefits of unconventional learning methods.

- Pilot Programs: Implement pilot programs to demonstrate the effectiveness of new approaches and build confidence in their scalability and impact.
- Incentives for Adoption: Provide incentives for educational institutions and educators to adopt and innovate in unconventional learning methods, such as grants, awards, and professional recognition.
- By addressing these challenges and leveraging the opportunities, NEP-2020 aims to create a more inclusive, flexible, and diverse education system that caters to the needs and aspirations of all learners.

CHAPTER4 CO-PO ATTAINMENT, ASSESSMENT OF DELIVERY OF EDUCATION

4.1 CO-PO ATTAINMENT, ASSESSMENT OF DELIVERY OF EDUCATION

Components of Assessment of Delivery of Education

Assessment of the delivery of education involves evaluating various components to ensure that educational objectives are being met effectively. The assessment is a critical aspect of ensuring that students are achieving the desired learning outcomes. The key components of assessment include:

Learning Outcomes:

Course Outcomes (COs): Specific objectives that students are expected to achieve upon completing a course. COs are aligned with the overall program objectives and are usually measurable and observable.

Program Outcomes (POs): Broad objectives that a program aims to achieve, reflecting the knowledge, skills, and attitudes that graduates should possess. POs are often aligned with national and international standards.

Teaching Methods:

Instructional Strategies: The methods and techniques used by educators to deliver content and facilitate learning. This includes lectures, experiential, discussions, hands-on activities, and multimedia resources.

Pedagogical Approaches: The underlying philosophies and approaches to teaching, such as constructivism, experiential learning, and student-centric learning.

Assessment Methods:

Formative Assessment: Ongoing assessments conducted during the learning process to provide feedback and guide instruction. Regular and continuous assessment throughout the learning process to provide feedback and guide instructional adjustments. Examples include tests, quizzes, oral examination, assignments, class interaction, seminars, workshop, and field wok.

Summative Assessment: Assessments conducted at the end of a learning period to evaluate overall student achievement and to measure the extent of student learning against predefined standards. Examples include final exams, projects, open book examination, graded assignment and standardized tests.

Feedback Mechanisms:

Student Feedback: Surveys, focus groups, and other methods used to gather student opinions on the quality of instruction and learning experiences.

Peer Review: Evaluations conducted by colleagues to assess the effectiveness of teaching practices and

materials. Involving students in assessing each other's work to promote collaborative learning and critical thinking.

Self-Assessment: Reflection by educators on their own teaching practices and effectiveness. Encouraging students to reflect on their own learning and identify areas for improvement.

Performance-Based Assessment: Using tasks that require students to demonstrate their knowledge and skills in practical or real-world contexts.

Standardized Testing: Utilizing uniform tests to evaluate and compare the performance of students across different regions or institutions.

Learning Environment:

Physical Environment: The classroom setup, facilities, and resources available to support learning.

Digital Environment: Online platforms and digital tools used to enhance learning and provide flexible access to educational content.

4.2 Significance of CO and PO

Course Outcomes (COs) and Program Outcomes (POs) are critical for ensuring the quality and relevance of educational programs. The significance of CO and PO lies in their ability to:

- Ensure alignment between teaching, learning and assessment methods.
- Facilitate continuous improvement in educational programs by identifying areas that need enhancement.
- Provide a clear and transparent framework for evaluating student performance and program effectiveness.
- Stating what you want your students to be able to do at the end of the program?
- Assessing the students whether they are able to do what they are expected to do.
- Orienting teaching and other academic processes to facilitate students to do what they are expected to

do.

- Program outcomes (POs) of an engineering UG program, as per NBA, are indicated below.
- [i] **Engineering knowledge**: Apply the knowledge of mathematics, science, engineering fundamentals, and an engineering specialization to the solution of complex engineering problems.
- [ii] **Problem analysis**: Identify, formulate, review research literature, and analyze complex engineering problems reaching substantiated conclusions using first principles of mathematics, natural sciences, and engineering sciences.
- [iii] **Design/development of solutions**: Design solutions for complex engineering problems and design system components or processes that meet the specified needs with appropriate consideration for the public health and safety, and the cultural, societal, and environmental consideration
- [iv] **Conduct investigations of complex problems**: Use research-based knowledge and research methods including design of experiments, analysis and interpretation of data, and synthesis of the information to provide valid conclusions.
- [v] **Modern tool usage**: Create, select, and apply appropriate techniques, resources, and modern engineering and IT tools including prediction and modelling to complex engineering activities with an understanding of the limitations.
- [vi] **The engineer and society**: Apply reasoning informed by the contextual knowledge to assess societal, health, safety, legal and cultural issues and the consequent responsibilities relevant to the professional engineering practice.

- [vii] **Environment and sustainability**: Understand the impact of the professional engineering solutions in societal and environmental contexts, and demonstrate the knowledge of, and need for sustainable development.
- [viii] **Ethics**: Apply ethical principles and commit to professional ethics and responsibilities and norms of the engineering practice.
- [ix] **Individual and team work**: Function effectively as an individual, and as a member or leader in diverse teams, and in multidisciplinary settings.
- [x] **Communication**: Communicate effectively on complex engineering activities with the engineering community and with society at large, such as, being able to comprehend and write effective reports and design documentation, make effective presentations, and give and receive clear instructions.
- [xi] **Project management and finance**: Demonstrate knowledge and understanding of the engineering and management principles and apply these to one's own work, as a member and leader in a team, to manage projects and in multidisciplinary environments.
- [xii] **Life-long learning**: Recognize the need for and have the preparation and ability to engage in independent and life- long learning in the broadest context of technological change.

Program Educational Objectives [PEOs] are based on Why does Program exist. What is its specific relevance?

It describes the program specific achievements of graduates within first few years of their graduation from the program.

The PEOs, may be guided by global and local needs, vision of the Institution, long term goals etc.

For defining the PEOs the faculty members of the program must continuously work with all stakeholders: local employers, industry, students and the alumni.

Process for defining PEOs are based on

- Feedback format for collecting data from Stake holders.
- A process by which PEOs are created and reviewed periodically.
- A process by which the curriculum is created to meet the stated PEOs.
- A process to evaluate to what extent PEOs are attained.
- Review, Mid correction, and Continuous Quality Improvement.

Program outcomes

POs are statements about the knowledge, skills and attitudes (attributes) the graduate of a formal engineering program should have.

POs are defined by Accreditation Agencies of the country (NBA in India).

PEO – PO Matrix

- One can have 4-5 PEOs.
- All PEOs should be mapped to all 12 POs.
- Create a matrix to describe this mapping so that none of the POs are left out.
- Each PO is attained through program specific courses.
- The entry in the cell [0,1,2,3] indicates the level of correlation.
- The level of correlation in the matrix given below is only indicative.

PEO	PO1	PO2	PO3	PO4			PO10	PO11	PO12
1	1	2					3		1
2		3	1	2				2	
3	1				2				
4	3						2		3

Graduates of UG program in Mechanical Engineering will be able to :

- Engage in design and operation of systems, tools and applications in the field of mechanical engineering and allied engineering industries.
- Apply the knowledge of mechanical engineering to solve problems of social relevance, pursue higher education and research.
- Mechanical engineering graduates will work effectively as individuals and as team members in multidisciplinary projects.
- Engage in lifelong learning, career enhancement

and adopt to changing professional and societal needs.

CO-PO relationship

Each CO can be identified to address a subset of POs.

- Based on the number of COs and the sessions dedicated to them it is possible to identify the strength of mapping (1, 2 or 3) to POs.

- Based on these strengths of selected POs a CO-PO matrix can be established.

CO Attainment

- The assessments should be in alignment with the Cos.
- Question paper should be so set to assess all Cos.
- The average marks obtained in assessments against items for each CO will indicate the CO attainment.
- Instructors can set targets for each CO of his/her course.
- Attainment gaps can therefore be identified.
- Instructor can plan to reduce the attainment gaps or enhance attainment targets.
- All POs can be adequately addressed through the selection of core courses and their COs.

- Attainable targets can be selected for each of the CO.
- If assessment is in alignment with COs the performance of the students indicates the CO attainment.
- These measurements provide the basis for continuous improvement in the quality of learning.

4.3 CO-PO Attainment Calculation

Calculating CO-PO attainment involves measuring the extent to which students have achieved the specified outcomes. It establishes a matrix that links each CO with relevant POs to ensure alignment and coherence in the learning objectives.

Correlation Matrix: Creating a matrix that maps each CO to the relevant POs, indicating the degree of correlation between them.

Assessment Data Collection: Gathering data from various assessments, assignments, projects, and exams to evaluate student performance against the set indicators.

Direct Assessment: Collecting data from exams, assignments, projects, and other direct measures of student performance.

Indirect Assessment: Gathering data from surveys, self-assessments, and other indirect measures to complement the direct assessment data.

Score Aggregation: Aggregating scores from various assessments to calculate the attainment levels for each CO.

Weighted Average: Using a weighted average approach to calculate PO attainment based on the contribution of each CO to the PO.

Threshold Levels: Setting threshold levels for acceptable attainment of COs and POs to identify areas needing improvement.

Benchmarking: Comparing attainment levels against benchmarks or standards to assess overall performance.

4.4 Opportunities:

The implementation of CO-PO attainment-assessment in the delivery of education presents several opportunities:

Enhanced Learning Outcomes: Clear and measurable COs and POs guide students towards achieving specific learning goals, leading to better educational outcomes.

Continuous Improvement: Regular assessment and feedback enable continuous improvement in teaching methods, curriculum design, and student support services.

Accountability and Transparency: A systematic approach to assessment ensures accountability and transparency in the education system, building trust among stakeholders.

Personalized Learning: Data-driven insights from

CO-PO assessments allow for personalized learning

plans that cater to the individual needs and strengths of students.

Targeted Improvement: Identifying specific areas where students are struggling allows for targeted interventions to **IMPROVE LEARNING OUTCOMES.**

Innovative Methods: The focus on outcomes encourages the adoption of innovative teaching methods and technologies to enhance student learning.

Stakeholder Trust: Transparent assessment processes build trust among stakeholders, including students, parents, and accreditation bodies.

4.5 Challenges:

Despite the benefits, there are several challenges associated with CO-PO attainment and assessment:

Complexity in Implementation: Mapping COs to POs and setting appropriate performance indicators can be complex and time-consuming.

Data Management: Collecting, analysing, and managing large volumes of assessment data requires robust systems and skilled personnel.

Resistance to Change: Educators and institutions may resist changes to traditional teaching and assessment methods, hindering the adoption of CO-PO frameworks.

Resource Constraints: Implementing comprehensive assessment systems requires significant resources, including time, money, and technology, training, and support services.

Consistency: Ensuring consistency in assessment methods and data collection across different courses and programs can be challenging.

Training Needs: Adequate training and support are required to help educators adapt to new assessment practices and technologies.

Infrastructure: Developing the necessary infrastructure for data collection, storage, and analysis can be resource-intensive.

Holistic Assessment: Balancing the use of quantitative data (scores, metrics) with qualitative data (feedback, observations) is essential for a holistic assessment.

Subjectivity: Qualitative assessments can be subjective, making it challenging to ensure consistency and fairness.

4.6 Possible Solutions:

To address these challenges, the following solutions can be considered:

Professional Development: Providing training and support to educators on CO-PO frameworks, assessment methods, and data analysis techniques.

Technology Integration: Utilizing technology to streamline data collection, analysis, and reporting processes, making assessment more efficient and effective. Integrate CO-PO attainment tracking into LMS to automate data collection and provide real-time insights

Stakeholder Engagement: Involving all stakeholders, including educators, students, and parents, in the development and implementation of CO-PO assessment systems to ensure buy-in and support.

Resource Allocation: Allocating sufficient resources to develop and maintain robust assessment systems, including investing in technology and professional development.

Support Networks: Establish support networks and communities of practice for educators to share best practices and collaborate on assessment strategies.

Infrastructure Development: Invest in developing the necessary infrastructure for data collection, storage, and analysis to support effective assessment practices.

Mixed Methods: Use a combination of quantitative and qualitative assessment methods to provide a balanced and holistic evaluation of learning outcomes.

Standardization: Develop standardized guidelines and rubrics for qualitative assessments to ensure consistency and fairness.

By leveraging these opportunities and addressing the challenges, NEP-2020 aims to create an education system that is focused on continuous improvement, accountability, and student success.

4.7 A Proposal for Calculation of CO-PO Attainment

- When Bloom's Level [BL] of syllabus and BL of QP are different.
- Intelligent CO-PO Attainment model for misalignment in assessing BL & "instruction BL" is presented.
- The achievement of Learning Objectives is assessed after the course is delivered and is called Learning Outcome.
- CO-PO Attainment Level is the most significant parameter for Accreditation.
- Schools/ HEIs will be regularly/periodically graded on established quality parameters of education and Accreditation such as A;B;C;D etc.[or any other grading method].
- The Cap on admissible fee [maximum] will be different for each Group of Institution.
- The Universities can fix the admissible program fee under this CAP based on the accreditation grades.
- All fresh Ph.D. entrants will be required to take credit-based courses in teaching / education/ pedagogy/ writing related to their Ph.D. subject.
- HEIs will have the flexibility to offer different designs of master's programs.

Theory of Machines :(L-T-P as 3- 1- 0);Total Hrs= 36

SAMPLE SYLLABUS WITH BLOOM'S LEVEL

CO	Course Outcome	Syllabus		BL	Av BL
CO1	Understand the linkage mechanisms, Analyse their motion, Study the correlation between the 4- bar linkage and its inversion; Understand the calculation of velocity of any point in the Mechanism , Learn concept of Instantaneous center.	Unit I.1 Links types, Kinematics pairs classification, Constraint types, Degree of Freedom, Grubler's equation, linkage mechanisms		BL1 2Hrs	[BL1x2 + BL2x2+ BL3x3]/7 = 15/7 = BL2 7 Hrs
		Unit I.2 Inversions of four bar linkage, slider crank chain and double slider crank chain.		BL2 2Hrs	
		Unit I.3 Velocity in Mechanisms: Velocity of point in mechanism, relative velocity method instantaneous point in mechanism,		BL3 3Hrs	

		Kennedy's theorem, instantaneous center method.			
CO2	Understand about the various friction drives such as Clutches, Brakes and Dynamometers. Learn about their working; Learn about their classification and relative advantages.	Unit 2.1 Classification of clutches, torque transmission capacity, considerations for uniform wear and uniform pressure theory, single plate and multi-plate clutch, centrifugal clutch		BL1 3Hrs	[BL1x3 + BL1x3]/6 = 6/6 = BL1 6 Hrs
		Unit 2.2 Classification of brakes, Braking effect, Analysis of Brakes, Classification of Dynamometers.		BL1 3Hrs	
CO3		Unit 3.2 coefficient of fluctuation of speed and energy, Limiting velocity of flywheel		PO1; PO2	BL2 3Hrs

		Unit 3.3 Design of flywheels for engines and punching machines	PO1;PO2;PO3	BL4 3Hrs	
CO4	Understand about function of Governor & working principle; Calculate Controlling force; Analyse Characteristics of Governor; Study about Concept of isochronism, Sensitivity of governor, Characteristics of governors, Hunting of governors.	Unit 4.1 Necessity of governor, Classification of Governors, Working principle of centrifugal governors	PO1	BL1 3Hrs	[BL1x3+BL2x4+]/7=11/7=BL2 7Hrs
		Unit 4.2 Concept of control force, Control force diagram, Stability of governor, Condition for stability, Concept of isochronism, Sensitivity of governor, Characteristics of governors, Hunting of governors.	PO1;PO2	BL2 4Hrs	
CO5	Learn about Principle of gyroscope, active and reactive couples.	Unit 5.1 Principle of gyroscope, Definition of axes, active and reactive couples	PO1;PO2	BL2 3Hrs	[BL2x3+

	Understand Rolling, Swaying and Pitching motions; Discuss Gyroscopic effect in a rotor, two wheelers, Four wheelers, ship and airplane	UNIT 5.2 Rolling, Swaying and Pitching motions; Gyroscopic effect in a rotor, two wheelers, Four wheelers, ship and airplane	PO1;PO2;PO3	BL25Hrs	BL2x5+]/8=16/8=BL28Hrs
				36 Hrs	

Correlation Between COs and POs for the Course

Corelation Level	Indicating Digit
No Corelation	0
Mild Corelation	1
Moderate Corelation	2
Strong Corelation	3

CO1 – PO1 relationship = [2+2+3 Hrs]x 3/7 = 3

CO1 – PO2 relationship = [3 Hrs]x 3/7 = 9/7 = 1

CO2 - PO1 relationship = [3+3 Hs] x 1/6 = 1

CO3 – PO1 relationship = [2+3+3 Hrs]x 3/8 = 3

CO3 – PO2 relationship = [3+3 Hrs]x 3/8 = 18/8 = 2

CO3 – PO3 relationship = [3 Hrs]x 3/8 = 9/8 = 1

CO4 – PO1 relationship = [3+4 Hrs]x 3/7 = 3

CO4 – PO2 relationship = [4 Hrs]x 3/7 = 12/7 = 2

CO5 – PO1 relationship = [3+5 Hrs]x 3/8 = 3

CO5 – PO2 relationship = [3+5 Hrs]x 3/8 = 3

CO5 – PO3 relationship = [5 Hrs]x 3/8 = 15/8 = 2

Course Name : Theory of Machines [ToM]

CO	Program Outcomes [PO ; PSO]													
				PO4	PO5	PO6	PO7	PO8	PO9	PO10	PO11	PO12	PSO1	PSO2
ToM.CO1														
ToM.CO2														
ToM.CO3														
ToM.CO4														
ToM.CO5														
Average														

MAPPING CORRELATION BETWEEN COURSE NUMBER AND POs – WIJ

Course Number/Name	Program Outcomes [PO ; PSO]														
	1		[illegible]											PSO1	[illegible]
1. To M	2.6		[illegible]												
2. F M	3		[illegible]												
3. PHY	3														
4. CHE	3														
5. MAT	3														
6. *****			[illegible]												
7. *****	2		[illegible]											3	[illegible]
8. *****	2														
9. *****	3														
10.*															

***															
******														3	2
******															3
38.****	1														
39.****	1														
40.****															
Average	*		*											*	*

Share of Direct & Indirect Assessment

Assessment of CO attainment is carried out in TWO modes: **Directly** [actual marks basis] & **Indirectly** [Feedback on perspective basis]. The ratio of Direct assessment to Indirect assessment of CO attainment could be 80%: 20% or otherwise as per University Rules.

S. No.	TOOL	CATEGORY
1.	CO Attainment of all theory and Lab courses(Sessional examination, Assignments and End Semester Examination)	Direct Assessment (70%- 80%)
2.	Indirect Assessment : Course wise student and Teachers feedback (during end semester exam)	Indirect Assessment. (30% - 20%)

Each Course generally has two types of Examinations:

1 Carried out by teacher himself: also called Sessional Examination, Internal Examination.

2 Carried out by External Examiner: also called External Examination; End Semester Examination; Final Examination.

The CO attainment targets Y and X naturally should be fixed differently.

LEVEL	Internal Examination Y = 70	External Examination X = 50
Level 1	40% to 50% students scoring more than Y% marks [40;50]	40% to 50% students scoring more than X% marks [40;50]
Level 2	50% to 60% students scoring more than Y% marks [50;60]	50% to 60% students scoring more than X% marks [50;60]
Level 3	>=60% students scoring more than Y% marks [>=60]	>=60% students scoring more than X% marks [>=60]

COURSE ATTAINMENT LEVEL RUBRICS

Evaluation Component	Value of X or Y
Assignment (Write Assignments/ Mini Projects/ Flipped Classes/ Lab Quizzes/ Practice sheets	80% Marks
Mid Semester/Sessional Examinations	60% Marks
End Semester Examinations	50% Marks
Project Work/ Internships	75% Marks
% Student meeting criteria	Level attainment on the basis of Criteria X
Above 60% meeting the criteria (X)	3
Between 60% to 50% criteria (X)	2
Between 50% to 40% Criteria (X)	1
Less than 40% Criteria (X)	0

Finding CO Attainment for one Course – [say Theory of Machines]

- The proportional weightages of Continuous Internal Assessment and End Semester Examination [CIE: ESE] will be as per the academic regulations in force.
- Proportions of 20:80, 25:75, 30:70, 40:60, 50:50 are all possible.
- Let us denote this ratio as C:E

Indirect attainment

- Feedback on Curriculum from Final year Students (Graduating) – 10%.
- Feedback on Curriculum from Teachers -10%.
- Feedback on Curriculum from HR/Employers of Students 10%
- Feedback of External Mentors from Industry-10%.
- Feedback on Curriculum from Alumni -20%.
- Feedback from Co-curricular Activities- 40% may be included in Indirect attainment.

Direct attainment

- Question paper should be set to assess all COs in alignment with the BL levels prescribed in the syllabus.
- Attainable targets "X" can be selected for all the CO by Instructors/ Teachers in accordance with the University Policy.
- After computing attainment Levels, attainment gaps can be identified. Instructor can plan to reduce the attainment gaps or enhance attainment targets.
- If there is mis-match between BL of syllabus and BL of QP, then correction measures need to be taken

to compute CO Attainment Levels.

- Computation of Direct Assessment in ESE.
- Defining POs for each program based on Graduate Attributes.

CO	Syllabus	PO	BL	AvBL	MM	AvBL	BL	MM	AvBL
CO1	Unit I.1	PO1	BL1 2Hrs	BL2 7Hrs	4	[BL1x4+BL2x6+BL3x10]/20=46/20=BL2.3	2	4	[BL2x4+BL2x6+BL3x10]/20=50/20=BL2.5
	Unit I.2	PO1	BL2 2Hrs		6		2	6	
	Unit I.3	PO1.PO2	BL3 3Hrs		10	=BL2.3	3	10	=BL2.5
CO2	Uni	PO1	BL1	BL1	10	[BL	1	10	[BL

	t2.1		3Hrs	6Hrs		1x10+BL1x10]/20=20/20=BL1			1x10+BL2x10]/20=30/20=BL1.5
	Unit2.2	PO1	BL13Hrs		10		2	10	
CO3	Unit3.1	PO1	BL32Hrs	BL3 8Hrs	10	[BL3x10+BL2x2+BL4x8]/20=66/20=B	3	10	[BL3x10+BL1x2+BL4x8]/20=64/20=B
	Unit3.2	PO1;PO2	BL23Hrs		2		1	2	
	Unit3.3	PO1;PO2;PO3	BL43Hrs		8		4	8	

						L3.3			L3.2
CO4	Unit4.1	PO1	BL13Hrs	BL2 7Hrs	10	[BL1x10+BL2x10]/20=30/20=BL1.5	2	10	[BL2x10+BL2x10]/20=40/20=BL2
	Unit4.2	PO1;PO2	BL24Hrs		10		2	10	
CO5	Unit5.1	PO1;PO2	BL23Hrs	BL28Hrs Av2	10	[BL2x10+BL2x10]/20=40/	2	10	[BL2x10+BL3x10]/20=50/
	UNIT5.2	PO1;PO2;PO3	BL25Hrs		10		3	10	

						20=BL2 Av2.02			20=BL2.5Av2.34

Defining COs for each course of the program under the umbrella of POs: (CO- PO Correlation).

- The COs for each course should match with the 5 Units of the Course Syllabus.
- Defining the Degree of difficulty BL for each Unit of the Course at which it is taught (to be included in the syllabus).
- Deciding share of Direct and Indirect assessment in computing CO Attainment Level.

- Deciding the Target values of X (for theory) and Y (for internal marks) in CO Attainment Level calculation.
- Correlating the Degree of difficulty BL for each Unit of the Course at which it is taught vs BL level of the question asked in the QP.
- The range of Bloom's Level is 1-6 and that of Assessment Level is 1-3.
- BL level of any question has a strong Correlation with marks of the question in determining Attainment level of CO.
- Calculation of weighted average may be acceptable.
- Syllabus format to be modified to accommodate COs and BLs.

Question Paper Another Sample Template (with Internal Choice)							
Question Number	CO	BL Level BL	Max Marks MM	Average BL	BL	MM	Average BL
Q1 I	CO1	2	2	[BL2x2x2+ BL2x8x3]/28 =56/28 =BL2	2	2	[BL2x2x2+ BL3x8x3]/28 =80/28 =BL2.86
Q1 II	CO1	2	2		2	2	
Q1 III	CO1	2	8		3	8	
Q1 IV	CO1	2	8		3	8	
Q1 V	CO1	2	8		3	8	
Attempt Any two parts out of III, IV, V of 8 marks each							
Q2 I	CO2	1	2	[BL1x2x2+ BL1x8x3]/28 =28/28 =BL1	1	2	[BL1x2x1+ BL2x2x1+ BL1x8x1+ BL2x8x2]/2
Q2 II	CO2	1	2		2	2	
Q2 III	CO2	1	8		1	8	

Q2IV	CO2	1	8		2	8	=46/28 =BL 1.64
Q2V	CO2	1	8		2	8	
Attempt Any two parts out of III, IV, V of 8 marks each							
Q3I	CO3	3	2	[BL3x2x2+ BL3x8x3]/28 =84/28 =BL3	3	2	[BL 3x2 x2+ BL4 x8x 2+ BL3 x8x 1]/28 =100/28 =BL 3.57
Q3II	CO3	3	2		3	2	
Q3III	CO3	3	8		4	8	
Q3IV	CO3	3	8		4	8	
Q3V	CO3	3	8		3	8	
Attempt Any two parts out of III, IV, V of 8 marks each							
Q4I	CO4	2	2	[BL2x2x2+ BL2x8x3]/28 =56/28 =BL2	2	2	[BL 2x2 x2+ BL2 x8x 2+ BL1 x8x 1]/28 =48/28 =BL 1.71
Q4II	CO4	2	2		2	2	
Q4III	CO4	2	8		2	8	
Q4IV	CO4	2	8		2	8	

Q4V	CO5	2	8		1	8	
Attempt Any two parts out of III, IV, V of 8 marks each							
Q5I	CO5	2	2	[BL2x2x2+ BL2x8x3]/28 =56/28 =BL2	2	2	[BL 2x2 x2+ BL2 x8x 1+ BL3 x8x 2]/2 =72/ 28 =BL 2.57
Q5II	CO5	2	2		2	2	
Q5III	CO5	2	8		2	8	
Q5IV	CO5	2	8		3	8	
Q5V	CO6	2	8		3	8	
Attempt Any two parts out of III, IV, V of 8 marks each				Av BL2	Av BL2.47		

Question Paper: Theory of Machines
Max Marks : 100

Factor for modification of Target "X" = 2.0 /2.34

- If our target X = 50 marks in theory paper, then modified target will be = 50 *2.0 /2.34 = 43 marks. THE TARGER "X" IS REVISED FROM 50 TO 43.
- Factor for modification of "X" = 2.0 /2.47
- If our target X = 55 marks in theory paper, then modified target will be = 55 * 2.0 /2.47 = 45 marks. THE TARGER "X" IS REVISED FROM 55 TO 45.

FINAL CALCULATIONS

[Direct Attainment] = E * [External Assessment] + C*[Continuous Internal Assessment]

[Indirect Attainment] = Course Survey/Feedback

Course Attainment Level COi = DA*0.8 + IA*0.2

ATTAINMENT LEVELS OF Course Outcome COi

S.No.	Levels	Quality of Performance
1	COi ≤ 1	Unsatisfactory
2	1 ≤ COi ≤ 1.5	Satisfactory
3	1.5 ≤ COi ≤ 2.5	Good
4	2.5 ≤ COi ≤ 3.0	Excellent

Calculation of Attainment Level of jth Program Outcome = Pj

- If Ci = Credit [weightage] of ith Course in the program structure; Wij= Corelation Level of ith course with jth Program Outcome.
- CAi = Course Attainment Level of ith Course Question
- Average Attainment Level of jth Program Outcome
- Pj = ∑ Ci * CAi * Wij / ∑ Ci * Wij
- for j = 1,2.3 …., 12, and i= 1,2,3, ….., 40
- P1 = {(C1*CA1*2.6)+(C2*CA2* 3) +(C3*CA3*3)+ ….+(C40*CA40* 0) / ∑ Ci* Wij
- Calculation of Average PO Attainment Level
- PA = Average Program Attainment Level for all 12 POs.
- Pj = Attainment Level of Jth PO.
- PA = Σ Pj / n for J=1,2,3….n and n=12

CALCULATION OF PEO ATTAINMENT LEVEL

- PEOi = Average Attainment Level of ith PEO

- P_j = Attainment Level of Jth PO
- where, j=1,2, 3,… 12 and PO includes PSO
- CW_{ij} = Correlation Weightage of ith PEO with jth PO
- $CW_{24} = 2$
- $PEO_i = \Sigma\, CW_{ij} * P_j / n$

CHAPTER-5 DESIGN OF PROGRAM STRUCTURE

5.1 PHILOSOPHY OF PROGRAM STRUCTURE DESIGN:

The philosophy behind designing a program structure

is to create an educational framework that is flexible, inclusive, and adaptable to the diverse needs of students. It aims to provide a holistic learning experience that integrates academic knowledge with practical skills, critical thinking, and personal development. Key principles include:

- **Flexibility**: Allowing students to choose courses and subjects that align with their interests and career aspirations. Offering multiple entry and exit points, a variety of course options, and personalized learning paths to accommodate different learning styles and career goals.

- **Interdisciplinarity:** Encouraging the integration of knowledge across different disciplines to foster a well-rounded education that transcends traditional boundaries. Motivating students to explore connections between different fields, fostering innovative thinking and problem-solving skills, that promotes critical thinking and problem-solving skills.
- **Student-Centric Approach:** Designing programs that cater to the individual learning styles and pace of students. Main emphasis on providing students with choices in subjects, pace of learning, and modes of instruction to enhance engagement and motivation. Creating engaging and interactive learning experiences that stimulate curiosity and foster a love for learning.
- **Skill Development**: Focus on equipping students with relevant skills and competencies that enhance their employability in a rapidly changing job market.
- **Lifelong Learning** : Designing programs that support continuous learning and skill development throughout an individual's life. Providing opportunities for adult learners to re-enter the education system and update their skills.
- **Outcome-Based Education:** Focusing on the achievement of specific learning outcomes that are relevant to both academic and professional success.
- **Integration:** Encouraging the integration of multiple disciplines to provide a well-rounded education that promotes critical thinking and problem-solving skills.
- **Collaboration:** Fostering collaboration among

different departments and faculties to design courses that reflect the interconnectedness of various fields of study.

- **Practical Application:** Ensuring that the program structure includes practical components such as internships, projects, and hands-on experiences that prepare students for the workforce.
- **Industry Alignment:** Aligning courses with industry requirements and emerging trends to enhance employability and relevance in the job market.
- **Innovation:** Encouraging innovation in curriculum design, teaching methods, and assessment practices to keep the education system dynamic and responsive to change and provides flexibility to faculty to innovate in these processes.

5.2 Components of Program Structure:

A well-designed program structure consists of several key components that work together to provide a comprehensive educational experience:

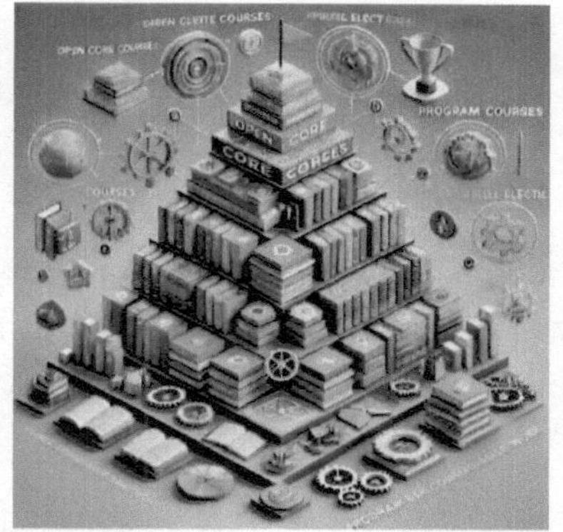

- **Open Core Courses:** Fundamental courses that provide essential knowledge and skills in various discipline. These courses are available at University level and are offered for a variety of programs to be taken as compulsory courses. They are mandatory for all students and cover the fundamental concepts of the discipline. Core courses ensure that all students have a solid understanding of essential concepts.

- **Program Core Courses:** These are program specific core courses and are offered for a specific program to be taken as compulsory courses. Based on the **Major** field of study, the student has to take these core courses.
- **Open Elective Courses:** Optional courses available at University level, that provide essential knowledge and skills in other disciplines. Elective courses allow students to tailor their learning experience according to their interests and career aspirations. They offer flexibility and enable students to explore different areas within the discipline. A variety of electives are offered to cater to diverse interests and career goals.
- **Program Elective Courses:** Courses that allow students to explore their interests in another specific areas within the discipline. Based on the **Minor** field of study the student can choose elective courses as per his choice.
- **General Education Courses:** General education courses cover a broad range of subjects, including humanities, social sciences, and natural sciences, to promote holistic development and a well-rounded education.
- **Practical/Field Work:** Practical components such as labs, workshops, internships, and projects provide hands-on learning opportunities that help students apply theoretical knowledge to real-world scenarios.
- **Projects:** They serve as culminating experiences that require students to integrate and apply their learning from different courses to address complex problems or create innovative solutions.
- **Skill Development Modules:** Courses or

workshops focused on developing essential skills such as communication, teamwork, and problem-solving, critical thinking, with a focus on enhancing employability.

- **Interdisciplinary Coursers**: Modules that combine elements from different disciplines to provide a holistic learning experience. Encouraging cross-disciplinary projects and research to foster innovation.
- **Assessment and Evaluation** : Using a variety of assessment methods, including formative and summative assessments, to evaluate student progress.
- **Feedback Mechanisms:** Providing timely and constructive feedback to support overall student development.

5.3 A Sample Design Procedure:

Designing a program structure involves a systematic procedure to ensure alignment with educational goals and student needs:

- **Needs Assessment:** Conducting surveys and consultations with stakeholders (students, faculty, industry) to identify the needs and expectations from the program and to understand industry trends, job market demands, and emerging fields of study. Engaging with stakeholders, including students, educators, industry professionals, and policymakers, will help identify educational needs and goals.
- **Defining Learning Outcomes:** Define the overarching goals and objectives of the program, including the knowledge, skills, and attitudes students are expected to acquire. Develop specific learning outcomes for each course and component of the

program, ensuring alignment with the overall program goals, including both academic knowledge and practical skills. Ensuring that program outcomes align with national and

international educational standards.

- **Curriculum Design**: Select core, elective, and specialization courses that align with the program goals and learning outcomes. Develop detailed course

content, including syllabi, learning materials, and assessment methods. Incorporate skill development modules, including vocational and technical training.

- **Program Structure** : Finalising the Courses, Course Credits, Design Program Structure of the Program including sequencing and timeline.
- **Course Design:** Developing detailed syllabi for each course, including objectives, content, teaching methods, and assessment strategies.
- **Integration of Components:** Ensuring that the core, elective, general education, and practical components are well-integrated and support each

other. Partner with industry to design practical components such as internships, industry projects, and workshops that provide real-world experience.

- **Continuous Evaluation:** Implementing mechanisms for regular review and improvement of the program based on feedback and performance data.
- **Feedback and Revision**: Implement the program on a pilot basis to gather feedback from students and faculty. Use the feedback to make necessary revisions and improvements to the program structure.

5.4 OPPORTUNITIES:

The design of an effective program structure offers several opportunities:

- **Enhanced Student Engagement:** A well-structured program can increase student motivation and engagement by aligning with their interests and career goals. Focus on skill development enhances employability and prepares students for the demands of the modern workforce. Incorporating practical components and interactive teaching methods increases student engagement and motivation. Focus on skill development prepares students for the demands of the modern workforce.
- **Improved Employability**: Aligning educational programs with industry needs will enhance employability and career readiness. Providing hands-on training and real-world experience will prepare students for the workforce.
- **Industry Collaboration**: Collaborating with industry ensures that the program remains relevant and aligned with market demands.
- **Improved Learning Outcomes:** Clearly defined

and well-integrated program components can lead to better academic performance and skill acquisition.

- **Career Readiness:** Programs that include practical experiences and skill development prepare students for the workforce and increase employability.
- **Lifelong Learning:** A flexible and interdisciplinary program structure encourages lifelong learning and adaptability. Making education more accessible to diverse populations, including working professionals, adult persons and rural communities.

5.5 Challenges:

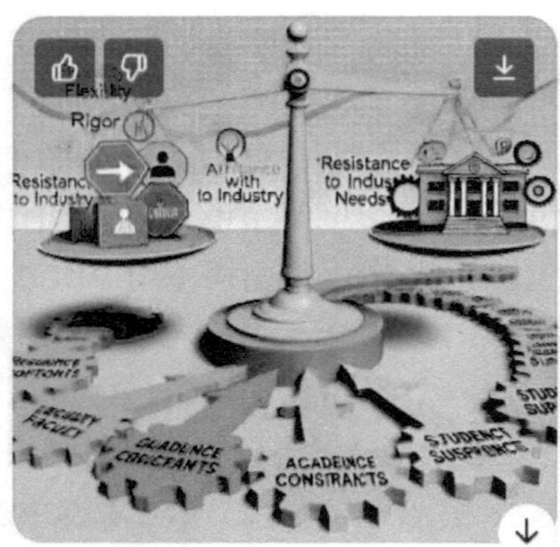

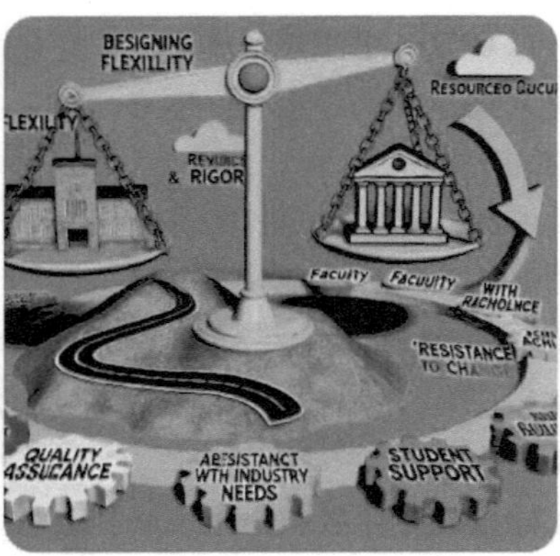

Despite the benefits, there are challenges in designing and implementing a program structure:

Balancing Flexibility and Rigor: Ensuring that the program remains rigorous while offering flexibility in course choices can be challenging. Designing flexible programs that still maintain academic focus and depth of knowledge. Balancing formative and summative assessments to accurately measure student learning outcomes. Providing flexibility offering choices to students, while maintaining a coherent and structured program can be challenging. It requires careful planning and coordination. Offering personalized learning paths requires robust student support services, including academic advising and career counselling.

- **Resource Constraints:** Developing and implementing a comprehensive program structure requires significant investment in resources, including faculty, facilities, and technology. Ensuring that the necessary infrastructure is in place to support practical components and interactive learning can be challenging.
- **Alignment with Industry Needs:** Continuously updating the program to align with evolving industry standards and job market demands can be difficult and impractical. Ensuring consistency and quality across different courses and components of the program can be difficult, especially in large and diverse institutions. Meeting accreditation requirements and maintaining high standards of quality and rigor is essential for the credibility of the program.
- **Resistance to Change:** Overcoming resistance from educators, institutions, and stakeholders accustomed to traditional education models. Providing sufficient training and support to faculty to adapt to new teaching and assessment methods.

• **Quality Assurance :** Developing robust evaluation and feedback mechanisms to continuously improve program quality. Ensuring consistency and quality across different courses and components of the program can be difficult, especially in large and

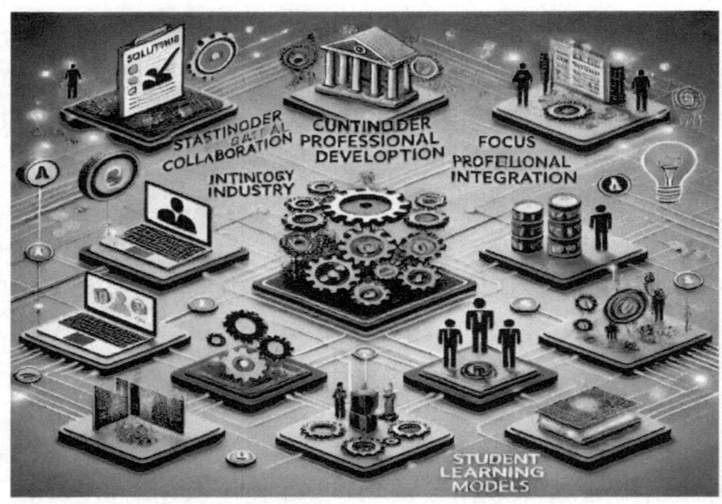

diverse institutions. Providing flexibility while maintaining a coherent and structured program can be challenging. It requires careful planning and coordination.

• **Student Support:** Providing adequate support and guidance to students in navigating the flexible program structure is essential but challenging.

5.6 Possible Solutions:

To address these challenges, the following solutions can be considered:

• **Stakeholder Collaboration:** Engaging with industry professionals, alumni, and other stakeholders to ensure the program remains relevant and aligned with job market needs. Partner with industry to share resources, expertise, and funding. Collaborative projects and internships can provide valuable real-world experience. Collaborate with other educational institutions to share best practices, resources, and innovative teaching methods.

- **Continuous Professional Development:** Providing faculty with ongoing training and support to effectively deliver the program and adapt to new educational methods.
- **Technology Integration:** Leveraging technology to enhance teaching and learning, streamline administrative processes, and provide flexible learning options. Use digital tools and platforms to enhance teaching, learning, and assessment. Online learning management systems can provide flexible and accessible learning options. Implement virtual labs and simulation tools to provide practical learning experiences without the need for extensive physical infrastructure.
- **Focus on Quality Assurance**: Adhere to accreditation standards and continuously monitor and evaluate the quality of the program. Implement a continuous improvement process that includes regular feedback from students, faculty, and industry stakeholders.
- **Student Advising and Support:** Establishing robust advising and support systems to help students navigate the program, make informed decisions, and achieve their goals. Implement mentorship programs that connect students with industry professionals and alumni for guidance and support.
- **Flexible Learning Models**: Adopt blended learning models that combine online and offline

learning experiences to provide flexibility and enhance engagement. Design modular courses that can be taken independently or as part of a larger program, allowing students to customize their learning experience.

By adopting these solutions, NEP-2020 aims to create a dynamic and effective program structure that supports student success and prepares graduates for the challenges of the future.

Design of Program Structure for B.Tech. Program

- It is the interconnected arrangement of Character-Building Courses, Co-curricular and Extracurricular activities, Passion and Hobby courses, Foundation, Core and Elective courses to include in Program Structure to accomplish predetermined objectives leading to the award of a degree.
- Different Courses, selected for the Program, may be listed in the form of a Matrix for the Program.
- The Degree of Corelation of CO with PO is also provided in the CO-PO Matrix.
- Proper assessment methods and tools are to be used at appropriate times to monitor and improve teaching-learning on a continuous basis.
- The assessment should be commensurate with the Bloom's Level of Depth of Learning.
- The assessment should be Learning Objective Oriented and not be randomly designed.

MAJOR

- The student chooses the Broad Area of Study in his UG as the Main Program and is advised to opt for Compulsory and Elective courses accordingly.
- These courses will lead to the award of UG degree

in some major field of study and are called **Major Courses**.

MINORS

- In order to do a **MINOR** in any field available in the University, a student is required to earn some additional credits, besides the credits of the main program.
- He is also required to fulfil the eligibility conditions of prerequisites for doing Minor.

SKILL ENHANCEMENT COURSES (SEC)

- Students, in all programs, are required to take up certain minimum credits of SECs, as prescribed, during the entire duration of the program.
- These courses will be Credit Courses, but no passing grade may be required in these courses. The grades earned will be included in the calculation of CGPA. Some SEC courses are indicated below:

Suggestive SEC
Online Certificate Programs
Certificate Programs conducted by Industry
Research Group (Seminars/ Conference/ Workshop)
Industry Supported Mini Projects
Certification in Industry related software
Tally/ Business Analytics/ NCFM (Beginners Module)/ NCFM/(Mutual fund Module)/ Training on Insurance Products
Plumbing/ Carpentry/ Wireman/ Electrician/ Fitter/ Mobile Repairing/ Electronics Goods Repairing/ Mobile Communication/ IP Network & Cyber Security/ Optical Fibre Technology
Trainings programs related to Industry viz. Automobile/ Pharmaceuticals/ Construction/ Electronics/ Hospitality/ Support service/ Engineering service sector
Soft skill development
Aptitude Development

INDUSTRY CERTIFICATE PROGRAMS

- In addition to the program credit courses, students can also opt for INDUSTRY CERTIFICATE PROGRAMS offered in-campus by the Industry as top up courses.

- There may be some kind of eligibility conditions, for being eligible to opt for these courses.

Industry Certificate Programs shall be **value added courses** like icing on the cake.

PASSION & HOBBY COURSES

- Every student will also have to **audit** minimum credits of **PASSION & HOBBY COURSES,** during the entire duration of the program.
- No regular grades may be awarded in such courses.
- If 'Satisfactory' grade is obtained in the course, the same will be reflected on the Grade sheet by the letter "S".
- Outstanding performers in these courses may also be awarded suitable certificates.
- These courses shall be delivered through Clubs, Communities, Societies, and Groups.
- These shall be formed, executed and managed by the students, under the supervision of faculty advisor.

Some such courses are indicated below:

Suggestive Passion & Hobby Courses
NCC, NSS, Yoga, Wellness club (Health Awareness club)
Music, Dance, Theatre, Poet's Club, Creative Writer's Club
Society for Education Upliftment among Poor Children
Women Empowerment Society, Old Age Help Group
Photography Club, Art Lovers Club, Journalism and Mass Com Club, Smile Community (Smile on the face of all stakeholders)
Advertising & Marketing society, Corporate Axis Community
HR Club (HR Development), Placement Help Group
Water Footprint Club (Awareness for water consumption)

Literature & Debate Society, Bloggers Society, I T Club
Flower Decoration, Alapana, Rangoli (Decoration club)
Volunteers / Activity Support Group
Incubation & Star Up Club, Robotics Club
Green Community (Environment Club)

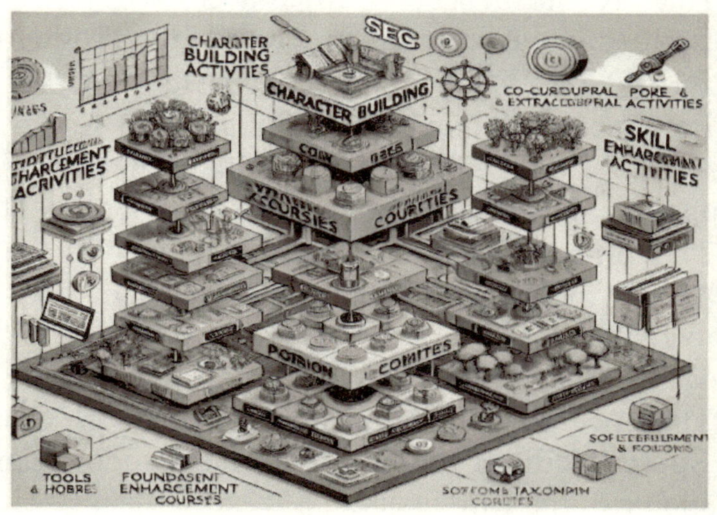

SPECIALISATION

- In some programs, the University may offer specialization, and the rules for opting them may be provided therein.
- The Faculty Advisor will guide him in choosing the specialization.

HONOUR'S PROGRAMS

- The University may offer a few Honour's programs in selected areas, which will be partly delivered by the Industry.
- These programs shall be in collaboration with the Industry and shall carry some extra credits as per the requirement of the specific Industry.
- The Faculty Advisor will guide him in choosing the specialization

SUMMER INTERNSHIP

- "Summer Internship/ Training in the Industry" may be treated as a Program Elective Course.
- Due credits shall be awarded accordingly to it, as prescribed in the program structure of the Program.

PRE-PLACEMENT INDUSTRIAL TRAINING

- Pre-placement industrial training/ Paid Internship (usually for one semester) in the final semester of the Program shall be admissible to the eligible students.
- The broad eligibility conditions, and details of delivery mechanism shall be decided by the University.

GAMES & SPORTS

- The students shall liberally participate in the Games & Sports facilities (both indoor and outdoor games) available in the University.
- However, credits shall be decided in the program structure.
- Outstanding performers in Games & Sports may also be awarded suitable certificates.

CHARACTER BUILDING COURSES

- To inculcate/ enhance the Concern and Respect for Human Values, Profession Ethics, Society & Community, Equity and National Pride, Environment & Ecology, Energy and National Concerns and Character Building, the students may be required to elect some minimum credits of such Courses.
- However, the minimum credits shall be decided in the program structure.

DESIGN OF PROGRAM STRUCTURE

National Education Policy focuses on:

- Recognizing the unique capability of each student,

- Flexibility of curriculum with no hard separation,
- Multidisciplinary and holistic education,
- Multiple exit/entry system using **Academic Bank of Credit,**
- Conceptual understanding, creativity and critical thinking rather than cramming,
- Inculcating value system, Life skills, Vocational and practical skills,
- Extensive use of technology, online, distance and adult education,
- Teacher's professional development and accreditation,
- Outstanding research,
- Formative assessment for learning,
- Sustainability issue,
- Quality education assessed through NAC,
- Learning Outcome based Education
- Pre-placement industrial training/ Paid Internship (usually for one semester) in the final semester of the Program shall be admissible to the eligible students.
- The Design of Program structure is being presented in **STEPS** for clarity. A sample example of **B. Tech Mechanical Engineering** program is taken to explain the procedure/ steps.

STEP – 1

Defining Credit & Fixing Course Credits

- Credit C = L + T + 0.5 P as per UGC
- L-T-P-C-H is Lecture-Tutorial-Practical-Credit-Contact Hours
- Common (L-T-P-C-H) are (0-0-2-1-2); (0-0-4-2-4); (1-0-0-1-1); (1-0-2-2-3); (2-1-2-4-5); (2-0-

3-4); (3-0-0-3-3); (3-1-2-5- 6); (3-2-2-6-7); (4-0-0-4-4); (4-0-2-5-6);(4-1-2-6-7);(5-0-0-5-5); (5-2-0-7-7)
Contact Hours/ week = Lecture credit + Tutorial credit + 2 *Practical credit

Example : L-T-P-C-H [3-1-2-5-6] i.e. H = 3 L+1 T+ (2*1P) = 6 Hr

STEP-2

Fixing Program Credits

• The UGC has suggested 13 to 15 working weeks per semester.

• Further, UGC has advised 18 to 20 credits per semester OR 36 to 40 credits per Year including all types of Academic Activities.

• Therefore 13 to 15 contact hours for Lecture/Tutorial OR 26 to 30 contact hours for Practical/ Field wok in a semester constitute ONE CREDIT.

Program	Duration	Total Credits
Certificate	One Semester	18 to 20
Advance Certificate	One Year	36 to 40
Diploma	Two years	72 to 80
Engg Diploma	Three years	108 to 120
UG	Three years	108 to 120
UG	Four years	144 to 160

• Say 4-year B.Tech Program will have Total **160** Credits.

STEP-3

Fixing Program Outcomes

• The Program Outcomes are decided before attempting to Design the Program Structure.

- Each Course MUST address to some Program Outcomes. CO-PO matrix helps in ensuring this point.
- All the COs of a course may address the same PO/PSO. Many will address PO1.

PO1: Engineering Knowledge

Possible that PO2, PO3, PO4, PO5 are addressed mildly by some COs.

PO2: Problem Analysis

PO3: Design/Development of Solutions

PO4: Conduct Investigations of Complex Problems

PO5: Modern Tool Usage

Very few courses address complex engineering problems.

Some specific courses, included in the Program, address PO7, PO8, PO9, PO10 and PO11.

PO7: Environment and Sustainability

PO8: Ethics

PO9: Individual and Teamwork

PO10: Communication

PO11: Project Management and Finance

Projects can potentially address many POs

Department can arrange for some activities outside the curriculum to address some POs

PO6: The Engineer and Society

PO12: Life-Long Learning; Self-learning

- Identify the Areas of Study in the Program – such as Applied Science, Humanities, Management, Engineering, Communication, General studies, Sports, Music, Hobby Courses, Value & Ethics etc.
- List, in each chosen area of study, ***as many courses as you(department) can*, in order of choice preference**, which in your opinion are offered in other

Universities & are important, and write down their names under the heading of specific Area of study. Thus, prepare an exhaustive list of courses.

- The **names of the courses could be similar** – such as Applied Physics & Engineering Physics, Engineering mechanics & Applied mechanics, which may have slightly different content (syllabus) to be prepared at a later stage.
- **Similar / same courses** – such as Optimization techniques- may be offered by **more than one department** – such as Mechanical Engineering, Mathematics and Management. They will be distinguished by their course codes. They may or may not have same course content (Syllabus). But there will be difference in the delivery/assessment of these courses by two or more different departments.
- Divide the courses into **CORE** courses (compulsory) and **ELECTIVE** courses (Optional) for the PROGRAM under consideration. For different Programs these CORE and ELECTIVE courses could be different.
- **CORE** courses are those, which the students MUST study in the PROGRAM.
- **OPEN** category courses are such courses, which students from **several different programs will study together.**
- **PROGRAM** courses are program specific courses and may/ may not be included in the list of **other programs.**
- In general, Applied Science, Humanities, Management, Communication & Language, Skilling, Hobby, Vocational Courses, Value Added Courses, Environment protection Courses, Courses on Ethics

may fall in OPEN category in Curriculum of any Program.

- In general, the Engineering courses/ Mechanical department courses will fall under **Program category.**
- However, general courses offered by Engineering departments- such as Non-conventional Energy systems, Environment studies, Linear programming, Introduction to Finite Elements techniques, Optimization techniques etc – may also fall in OPEN core/ Open elective category.
- Similarly, a course offered by **non- engineering departments** – such as Transformers and its applications (may be for Electrical engineering), Project Risk Management (may be for Civil engineering), may fall under **Program core/ Program elective category**.
- The Program will have 4 baskets of Courses namely: Program core; Program elective; Open core; Open elective
- The Program core will constitute the **Major Field of Study.**
- The Program Elective will constitute the **Minor Field of Study.**
- The Open core will consist of the compulsory courses on Computer coding, Value & Ethics, Life skills, Empathy, Respect for others, Cleanliness, Courtesy, Democratic spirit, Spirit of service, Environment courses, Character Building Courses.
- **The Open Elective** will consist of the Vocational courses, Skilling courses, Sports courses, Hobby courses, Passion courses, Music courses, Physical

education courses, the Arts and crafts courses.

- The suggested Credit distribution *may* be as given below:

Total Credits = 160. $\{X_1\ \% + X_2\ \% + X_3\ \% + X_4\ \%\} = 100\%$

Category	Description	Credit Distribution	Percentage
1.Program core	Major Field of Study	58 - 61	X1 % 36 – 38 %
2.Program Elective	Minor Field of Study	24 - 28	X2 % 15 - 17%
3.Open core	Computer coding, Value & Ethics, Life skills, empathy, respect for others, cleanliness, courtesy, democratic spirit, spirit of service Env, courses.	18 - 25	X3 % 12 – 14 %
4.Open Elective	Vocational; Skilling, Sports, Hobby, Passion, Music courses, Physical education, the Arts and crafts	52 - 56	X4 % 33- 35%

Step 4

Selection of Program Core Courses [58 to 61 credits]

Green – 1st Preference Blue - 2nd Preference RED- 3rd Preference

Name of Course	Sample Credit

	Green	Blue	Red
History of Engineering Sc.	1		
Engineering Mechanics		2	
Basic Mechanical & Civil Engineering.			2
Basic Electronics Engineering.			2
Basic Electrical Engineering			2
Computer Programming in C ++	2		
Engineering Graphics	2		
Engg. Drawing		2	
Basic Sciences [Phy, Math] -I	3		
Workshop Practice	2		
Manufacturing science – I	3		
Manufacturing Processes-II			2
Advanced Manufacturing Processes			2
Basic Sciences [Phy, Math] -II		2	

DESIGN OF PROGRAM STRUCTURE

Applied Thermodynamics	2		
I.C. Engines			2
Heat & Mass Transfer		2	
Refrigeration &Air Conditioning		2	
Automobile Engg.			2
Basic Economics, Finance course	2		
Strength Of Materials	2		
Kinematics of Machines		2	
Dynamic of Machines			2
Advanced Strength of Materials			2
Design of Machine Elements-I	3		
Design of Machine Elements-II			2
Computer Aided Engg. Design		2	
Basic Engg. Course	3		
Industrial Engg. & Management			2
Operations Research		2	
Mechanical Measurements	2		
Production Planning &Control			2
Material science & Engineering	2		

Fluid Mechanics	3		
Fluid Machines			2
Seminar	2		
Industrial Training	2		
Minor Project-I	2		
Project Work	6		
	4 4	**1 6**	**2 6**
	60		**2 6**

Step 5

Mapping Correlation Between Course Number and POs – Wij

Course Number	Program Outcomes [PO ; PSO]														
1.*****															
2.*****															
3.****															
4.*****															
5.*****															

6.*****															
7.*****															
8.*****															
9.*****															
10.****															
******															
******															

38.****															
39.****															
40.****															

- Identify the Areas of Study in the Program – such as Applied Science, Humanities, Management, Engineering, Communication, General studies, Sports, Music, Hobby Courses, Value & Ethics etc.
- Select the Courses from the list prepared, which can be offered.
- Assign L-T-P-C-H to each course in all the categories.
- Mark area of study against each course.
- Mark version 1.0 against each course. Version 1.0 indicates initial version of any course. Minor revision will be indicated by versions 1.1, 1.2, 1.3 .. .. Major changes in the syllabus of any course will be indicated by Version 2,3,4 ...
- Mark pre-requisites/ anti-requisites in the last column for the course, if any.
- Check that the pre-requisite conditions for the courses are satisfied.
- Moderate the positioning of the courses semester-

wise, LTPCH, etc as required for different semesters.

- Similarly prepare the Structure for **Program Elective, Open Core** and **Open Elective** Courses.
- Distribute them in different semesters based on their nature [Foundation, Fundamental, Pre-requisite requirements] in the **MODULAR FORM** to enable **multiple EXIT**.
- Prepare the Program Structure for all the Semesters.
- Check the total courses in PC, PE, OC, OE baskets based on credit requirement are balanced for all the semesters of the program.

CHAPTER-6 EVALUATION AND ASSESSMENT

6.1 PURPOSE OF ASSESSMENT

The three components of any educational system are: teaching, learning, and evaluation.

- We assess to know the depth and quality of learning that has happened.
- The current evaluation practices overlook the evaluation of student's critical understanding and the skills to apply the knowledge.

- The idea is to make assessment a learner-centric, learning friendly, having lots of fun, no pressure of examination, while judging the depth of learning in accordance with the Blooms level.
- In case of assessment of open distance learning courses, online learning courses, hobby courses, games & sports courses, many vocational courses the conventional assessment models may not give true results, and unconventional assessment tools have to be looked for.
- This is because of variation in the delivery of content, different learning objectives and learning methodologies adopted by students, the variety of assessors in the same course etc.
- For example, in cricket, a batter, a bowler, a keeper and a fielder all have different learning objectives and have to be assessed accordingly.

- Assessment must provide feedback to teacher as well as to the learner for improving the quality of learning.
- As such, the design of assessment model may be left to the choice of the assessor based on his competency.
- The assessor may be provided freedom and flexibility to choose any conventional or unconventional model of assessment.
- The system should measure the extent of acquisition of learning at target Bloom's level and help learners understand their learning competency.
- The examination process is similar to a quality control function in a manufacturing unit.
- Product with quality parameters below par are either reworked and rectified or rejected, if rework is not possible.
- Examination process follows 100% testing (evaluation) method.
- Therefore, contribution of assessment of student's learning is increasingly being emphasized in higher education to contribute to sustainable learning.

6.2 The Process of Learning

- Students come with a wide variety of abilities, attitudes, interests, ambitions, levels of motivation.
- The instructional methods that are effective for some students may be relatively ineffective for others.
- The process of learning consists of following steps:

STEPS	EXPLANATION
Motivation	The curiosity and eagerness in the learner to learn.
Apprehension	The perception of the learning material/source.

Acquisition	The co-relation of information/ knowledge to what he already knows.
Retention	The process of storing the information.
Recall	Retrieval of information when necessary.
Generalization	Developing strategies to process information for new situations.
Performance	Putting strategies into practice; Application of knowledge/ information.
Feedback	Feedback & Testing permits him to up-date knowledge from the results of his performance.

6.3 Learning Objectives

Learning objectives are explicit statements of what students should be able to do, when they have completed a segment of a course.

- **Learning objectives** can be particularly valuable if they are shared with the students, and then used as the basis of the test preparation.

- Having a proper set of learning objectives helps a teacher to decide on how much time to allocate to each topic/ plan lectures/ create relevant assignments/ and write relevant tests.
- They are presented in a tabular form below for ease of understanding.
- The different units/chapters of a course are often designed to be delivered at varying Bloom level [BL],

having an average BL for the entire course.

OBJECTIVES	EXPLANATION
Reading, Listening & Understanding	A low- level objective. Enables the student to read the text & understand the meaning of what he reads.
Retention & Recall	Retains & retrieves the relevant information when needed.
Assimilation	Understands what is not written explicitly. Can read/interpret between the lines.
Reasoning	Can reason out logically in a sequential manner on the topic he has learnt.
Analysis	Disintegrates the information for analysis. Learns why it is so.
Ideation	Imagination; Learns the process of generating ideas; New examples; New applications; Applications in other domains; Analogy.
Application/ Self- Learning	Application of knowledge/ information in new situation to which he was not exposed to earlier. Problem solving capability. Self-learning.

6.4 Teaching- Learning Techniques

- We learn through different processes.
- Every process has a different teaching- learning technique.
- Not everything can be learnt by a single method.
- Some of these techniques are:

TECHNIQUES	DETAILS	EXAMPLES
Expository	Expose students to new knowledge/ information. They learn from observation. Expose, and then explain. Sensing learners; Visual learners; Sequential learners	Explaining what a dam is; boiler; generator ; cat; dog; what is hot .

Explanatory	Explain the concept to student and make the student understand. Provide alternate explanation if he is not understanding	Demonstration/ classroom lecture/ question-answer session/ tutorial
Guided Discovery / Active learning (Getting the students to do things in class that actively engage them with the material being taught) Cooperative learning (Putting the students to work in teams under conditions that promote the development of teamwork skills while assuring individual accountability for the entire assignment)	This is student - centric approach; Let the student observe & reason out. Observation & logical reasoning often lead student to discover new knowledge. This is time consuming but very effective.	Seminars & mini projects; case studies; design problems
Experiential Type	Direct or simulated experience; use of support facilities- video & multimedia; industrial visits; labs.,	Observing during industrial visits followed by explanation. Doing experiments in labs,

		Video shows.
Exploratory Problem-based learning (Including project-based learning, inquiry-based learning, discovery-based learning, need-to-know learning, and just-in-time learning.)	Problem orientation; student learn through exploration. Self- Learning. Transfer & application of knowledge. (Teaching material may be provided only after a need to know has been established in the context of a complex question or problem, which increases the likelihood that the students will absorb and retain it). The teacher serves primarily as a consultant.	Major projects. New situations. Unconventional design problems. Using internet & google.
Denying a Fact	Negate a fact. Student learns to argue to justify his point and establish the fact. Develops logical reasoning capability.	Ex: Earth is not rotating. Sun does not rise from East. Inertia is not a Force.
Combination of two or more		

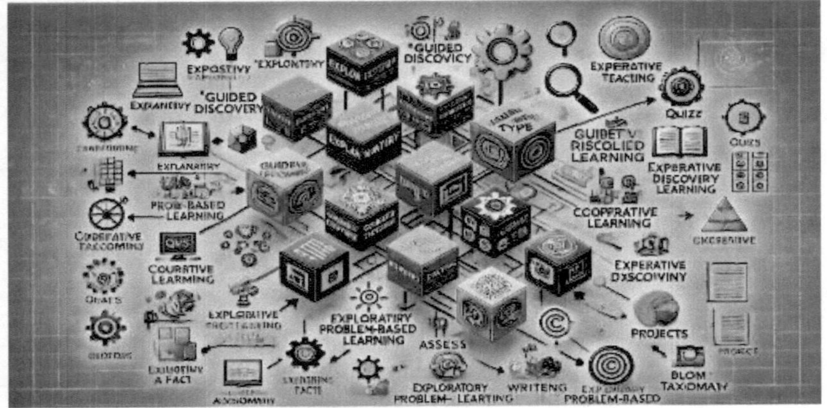

6.5 THE ASSESSMENT PROCESS:

- There are several modes through which we learn: every mode having its specific learning objectives. Everything cannot be learnt through a single process. (We cannot learn swimming through lecturing alone).
- Assessment is the direct testing of "**quality of learning**" and indirect testing of "**quality of teaching**".
- The various assessment tools include:

Assessment parameters	Description	Assessment objective	Bloom's level
Assignments	Short answers MCQ; Case studies; Problem related to applications; Practice	Understanding; application of knowledge; Student learning through exploration;	BL3

	numerical problems	Self-learning; Consolidation of key concepts;	
Quiz	MCQs; Multiple correct answers; Short answer questions	Memory & Recall; Reasoning; Analysis	BL4
Oral examination	Questions about key concepts; Discussion;	Understanding. Application	BL3
Written examination	Mathematical problems; Essay type questions; Short answer questions	Understanding; Cramming; Retention	BL1
Tutorials	Short answer questions; Numerical problems	Understanding. Ideation	BL3
Group Discussions	Discussion; Guided interaction	The ability to communicate; to organize thoughts; to interact with others; to reason and to analyse	BL4
Projects	The economy, society, and community are some	Developing ideas through guided discovery, exploration,	BL3

	areas of interest	applying the knowledge	
Simulation	Actual/ Virtual Simulation	Ideation; Analysis	BL4
Application and Analogy	Different areas of study utilize the same concepts/principles	Invention, exploration, discovery, & application of knowledge,	BL3
Essay/Long answer questions	The questions to answer in 15 minutes or more time; the numerical problems	Cramming, Organization, and Retention & Recall	BL1
Interaction during Expert Seminars	Experts from outside/from the faculty will conduct the seminar	Taking part in Q-A sessions and learning new concepts/ knowledge	BL1
Summary/Ab	Explanations that are brief	Compiling and condensing key points without	BL2

str act		sacrificing significance	
Interaction during Industry visit/ Tour	Visiting the workplace	Explaining; Understanding; Group activity;	BL3
Student Seminar, Presentation, Case study	Program/Course thrust areas	Communication; Exploration; Self-learning; Preparation & Presentation	BL2

6.6 Evaluation & Assessment of Learners:

Evaluation and assessment of learners are fundamental aspects of the educational process, ensuring that students achieve the desired learning outcomes. This involves various methods and

approaches to gauge student understanding, skills, and competencies:

Formative Assessment: Continuous assessment through quizzes, assignments, class participation, and feedback to monitor student progress in learning and provide ongoing support.

- **Summative Assessment:** End-of-term or end-of-course exams, projects, and presentations to evaluate student overall learning against predefined standards.
- **Diagnostic Assessment:** Pre-assessment to identify students' existing knowledge and skills.
- **Performance-Based Assessment:** Tasks that require students to demonstrate their knowledge and skills through practical applications.
- **Self and Peer Assessment:** Encouraging students to reflect on their own work and evaluate their peers' contributions to foster collaborative skills.
- Student assessment will be based on (i) Marks obtained in conventional exam. (ii) Self- Assessment

(iii) Peer Assessment (iv) Teacher Assessment.

- Examination in Open Distance Learning (ODL), Online programs, Traditional off-line programs have to be suitably designed to **Attain the desired Program outcome** in each case.

6.7 Evaluation & Assessment of Teachers:

Just as student performance is assessed, the effectiveness of teachers also needs regular evaluation to ensure high-quality education. This includes:

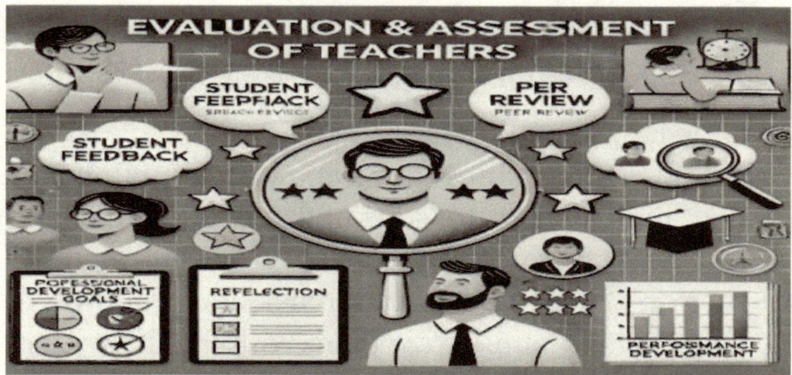

- **Student Feedback:** Collecting feedback from students on teaching methods, course content, and classroom environment.
- **Peer Review:** Having colleagues observe and evaluate teaching practices, providing constructive feedback and support.
- **Self-Assessment:** Encouraging teachers to reflect on their own teaching practices and identify areas for improvement.
- **Performance Metrics:** Using data on student performance, retention rates, and other relevant indicators to assess teacher effectiveness.

- **Professional Development Goals:** Setting and evaluating goals related to continuous professional growth and development.

6.8 Teacher's Training:

Continuous professional development and training are crucial for teachers to stay updated with the latest educational practices and technologies. This includes: **Induction Programs**: Comprehensive training for new teachers to familiarize them with the institution's policies, curriculum, and teaching methods.

- **Ongoing Professional Development:** Regular workshops, seminars, and courses to enhance teaching skills and knowledge.
- **Technology Integration:** Training on the effective use of educational technology.
- **Pedagogical Strategies:** Providing training on innovative and student-centric teaching methods.
- **Collaborative Learning:** Encouraging collaboration among teachers to share best practices, resources, and support.
- **Faculty Accreditation** may result in fixing differential salary package based on personal Accreditation Grades.

6.9 Opportunities:

Implementing effective evaluation and assessment practices presents several opportunities:

Improved Learning Outcomes: Regular and comprehensive assessment helps identify gaps in student understanding and provides opportunities for timely intervention.

- **Enhanced Teaching Practices:** Continuous evaluation and professional development for teachers lead to improved teaching methods and better student engagement.
- **Personalized Learning:** Data from assessments can be used to tailor instruction to meet individual student needs.
- **Accountability and Transparency:** Clear and consistent evaluation practices ensure accountability and transparency in the education system.

6.10 Challenges:

Despite the benefits, there are several challenges associated with evaluation and assessment:

- **Assessment Design:** Creating fair, reliable, and valid assessments that accurately measure student learning and teacher effectiveness can be complex.

- **Resource Constraints:** It requires significant resources, including time, money, and technology.
- **Resistance to Change:** Teachers and institutions may resist changes to traditional evaluation methods, hindering the adoption of new practices.
- **Data Management:** Collecting, analysing, and managing large volumes of assessment data requires robust systems and skilled personnel.
- With different choices of students of the same program, how timetable will be prepared suiting all the students.
- If we take any interesting course not needed in the program, how the grades are counted.
- Can one take playing cricket [batter] as a course. How relative evaluation will be done.
- What is audit course. Do we have FAIL grade in the course.
- Will all Vocational/skilling/hobby courses be credit courses and compulsory in all programs.
- How Adult programs will be offered and in which

mode- classroom mode or distance mode.

- Who will conduct online/ODL classes and how many courses of the program.

6.11 Possible Solutions:

To address these challenges, the following solutions

can be considered:

- **Professional Development:** Providing training and support to educators on assessment design, data analysis, and the use of technology in evaluation.
- **Technology Integration:** Utilizing technology to streamline data collection, analysis, and reporting processes, making assessment more efficient and effective.
- **Stakeholder Engagement:** Involving all stakeholders, including educators, students, and parents, in the development and implementation of evaluation systems to ensure buy-in and support.
- **Resource Allocation:** Allocating sufficient resources to develop and maintain robust evaluation systems, including investing in technology and professional development.

By leveraging these opportunities and addressing the challenges, NEP-2020 aims to create an education system that is focused on continuous improvement, accountability, and student success.

Unconventional Evaluations

- Unconventional assessment tools may be adopted for the evaluation of various components of assessment.
- In case of evaluating the answer books, a lot of time of the examiner is required, with no direct feedback to the students on the depth of learning.
- If the teacher wants to provide feedback on level of learning to the student, he needs to invest further time interacting with them on "one on one" basis.
- Further, one student does not know the strong and weak points of other students for the purpose of interaction and discussion on the topics with his classmates.
- For evaluating test/ quiz/ mid-term answer books, one may follow an unusual method.

1. Take the test/ quiz/ mid-term examination for say, one hour of the class students.
2. At the end, collect all the answer books with the roll number of the students written on them.
3. Redistribute all the answer books in the class randomly, one to each, so that no one gets his own answer book.
4. These students may write their roll number as the ***Student evaluators*** on the allotted answer book.
5. Then, the teacher should solve the examination questions in the class and discuss all the possible solution methods, explaining step-wise award of marks in each question.

6. Let the student evaluators award the marks on the allotted answer book for each question, as it is discussed in the class.

7. There may be incorrect/ faulty evaluations (lower or higher marks) ***intentionally*** on the basis of personal liking/dis-liking between the examinee and the student evaluator.

8. To check it, the teacher may announce in the class, before the start of the evaluation, that a few answer sheets shall be randomly selected and checked at the level of teacher. If some kind of intentional cheating is detected, that answer sheet shall be re-evaluated by the teacher himself, and 50% marks will be deducted as a *punishment for cheating* from the total marks obtained in the answer sheet of the ***faulty student evaluator.***

The proposed method, when followed in a class of 60 students, resulted in the evaluation of all the answer sheets within one hour of completion of examination with zero mistake. This way all the students will learn about :

- the step-wise award of marks discussed in the class,
- correct solution of all the questions of the test,
- involved in the process of evaluation of the answer sheet,
- besides completion of evaluation work in a very short time.

Group Viva-Voce:

- Generally, viva-voce examination of students in the lab class to know about the learning, requires a lot of time of the teacher if viva-voce is taken one-by-one.

- While, a question is asked from one student, others are indifferent to it, and do not listen and focus on the question.
- It becomes a session between two individuals, the teacher and one student.
- This results in unnecessary requirement of the extra time of the teacher, which could have been optimally utilised.
- Further, while the teacher is interacting with one student, this session may not be useful to others.
- In place of taking individual viva-voce examination, the practice of having ***Group Viva-Voce*** examination may be followed.
- One viva question may be announced in the class and 4 to 5 students may be permitted to answer one after the other in a sequence.
- Every student, besides answering the question, highlights the strong and weak points of the answer given be the previous student.
- Finally, the correct answer is provided to the class by the student or the teacher. Then, more questions are discussed in a similar manner.
- This way, the students know about the strengths and weaknesses of each other and later may interact among them.
- The teacher knows about the general difficulty of the class students, and improves teaching accordingly.
- The teacher assesses about the depth of learning of different topics by his class students.
- It helps him in awarding viva- voce marks/grades to his class students in a relative manner.
- A good number of questions can be discussed in the

class within the available time.

- The available class time is very effectively utilized, and lot of learning/ providing feedback happens.

Denying A Fact:

Another component of evaluation in different programs is *Seminar* given by students, wherein a student presents material on some advanced topic, collecting the information from research papers and/or available resources in public domain.

- The teacher and the students listen to the explanation given by him on the topic.
- The audience listens to the lecture and learns about the content presented by the speaker.
- Some unconventional assessment tools may be adopted for the evaluation of seminar presented by the speaker.
- One such method is by using ***Denying the Fact***.
- In this method anybody from the audience, including the students and the teacher, is permitted to ask questions negating some facts, thus, forcing the speaker to justify the fact.
- The speaker answers the query and justifies the fact presented by him.
- The audience sometimes, refuses to accept his

arguments and seeks alternate explanation on the query.

• The speaker rethinks and provides some alternate explanation on the query.

• In the process he struggles to give alternate arguments explaining his point and learns to strengthen his knowledge on the topic.

In this process :

• Audience has to concentrate on the matter presented by the speaker,

• The audience understands and learns the topic,

• The audience searches for the fact to be negated,

• The speaker learns the technique of satisfying the query,

• When requested to give alternate explanation, speaker learns to explain his point using alternate method,

• The depth of understanding the topic by the speaker and the audience, both, is improved,

• The teacher gets the opportunity of a wide spectrum of discussions to award suitable marks/grades to the speaker and the students who asked queries.

CHAPTER-7 QUALITY ASSURANCE, & GRADED ACCREDITATION

7.1 INTRODUCTION

Globalization has created uniformity in customer expectations world over. With the opening up of Indian economy, our industry sector has to compete globally even for the domestic market.

- This requires strong products with leading technology/quality and compelling cost advantage.
- Suitably trained manpower is critical to achieve this goal.
- Large pool of highly trained manpower has provided India leadership position in knowledge-based industries.
- Efforts are now required to translate this leadership in building indigenous manufacturing capabilities.
- Whereas China is already a leader in low-tech bulk manufacturing, India is emerging as leader in brain-intensive manufacturing.
- Present system, though huge and diverse, has focus on analytical abilities.
- This would require skill sets appropriate for

innovation, design, development and prototyping that too, using modern tools and techniques.

7.2 The ACCREDITATION

- The *Approval* of any Institution by the competent authority signifies the availability of land, building, equipment, and faculty necessary to carry out studies and deliver education in that institution.
- The availability of all the ***proper academic processes*** in the institute shows its preparedness to deliver the education to the students and is reflected by awarding ISO Certification to the willing institution.
- The approved institution with ISO Certification certifies only the availability of all process in place and not the Quality of education.
- The ***Quality of Delivery of Education*** to the students, achievement of educational objectives, competency building of students and their satisfaction and happiness level is adjudged in the ***Accreditation process.***
- The ***Accreditation*** of the institute is based on the quality of learning outcome, that the institute delivers with the available infrastructure, resources and the quality processes in place in the institute.
- Thus, whereas approval of the institute is based on the ***input*** infrastructure and resources available in the institute; the accreditation is based on the ***learning outcomes*** of the students delivered by the institute in providing quality education to its students, and transforming them into responsible citizens.
- ***Accreditation*** is the assurance of program quality.
- ***Accreditation*** is NOT any award system (like Gold,

Silver, 1,2,3,..), Nor any Investigation of a complaint, Nor a *Regulatory Process,* Nor an Audit, ***not even a ranking system.***

7.3 NEED FOR ACCREDITATION

- Students; Faculty; Support Staff; Industry and Employers; Parents; Society; Government all are the Stakeholders of the Institution, whom the institution has to satisfy. It shows Recognition by the stakeholders. It ensures Education Quality Assurance. It is needed for Branding and Marketing. It is needed for Global recognition of Graduates.
- Assurance that the institute provides all that is required inputs for a confident Graduate of tomorrow. Prepare a 21st Century Graduate.
- Assurance that understanding fundamentals very well, and learning new skills/competencies by the students, that would enable individuals to cope with the demands of the rapidly changing workplace
- 7.4 COMPONENTS OF QUALITY OF EDUCATION:

Quality assurance in education involves a comprehensive approach to ensure that educational institutions deliver high standards of teaching, learning, and student support. The key components include:

- **Curriculum Design:** Developing a curriculum that is relevant, up-to-date, and aligned with industry standards and societal needs.
- **Teaching Methods:** Employing innovative and effective teaching methodologies that cater to diverse learning styles and promote critical thinking.
- **Learning Resources:** Providing adequate learning resources, including libraries, laboratories, and digital tools, to support student learning.
- **Faculty Qualifications:** Ensuring that educators are highly qualified, experienced, and continuously engaged in professional development.
- **Student Support Services:** Offering comprehensive support services such as counselling, career guidance, and extracurricular activities to enhance student well-being and development.
- **Assessment and Evaluation:** Implementing robust assessment and evaluation processes to measure student learning outcomes and program effectiveness.

7.5 Process of Accreditation:

Accreditation is a formal process that evaluates and certifies the quality and standards of educational institutions. The process typically involves:

- **Self-Study:** Institutions conduct a thorough self-assessment to evaluate their strengths, weaknesses, and areas for improvement.
- **Submission of Reports:** Preparing and submitting detailed reports that provide evidence of compliance with accreditation standards.
- **Peer Review:** A team of external reviewers, usually comprising academic peers, visits the institution to assess its facilities, programs, and practices.

- **Feedback and Recommendations:** The review team provides feedback and recommendations for improvement based on their findings.
- **Accreditation Decision:** The accrediting body evaluates the reports and feedback to make a final decision on accreditation status.
- **Continuous Improvement:** Institutions are encouraged to continuously improve their practices based on the recommendations and maintain their accreditation status through regular reviews.

7.6 NAAC ACCREDITATION PROCESS:

The criteria- based quality assessment forms the backbone of any assessment and accreditation process. The seven criteria identified by NAAC represent the main functions and activities of a higher educational institution. In the revised framework not only the academic and administrative aspects of institutional functioning, but also the emerging issues have been included by NAAC. The seven Criteria to serve as basis for assessment of higher educational institutions are:

1. Curricular Aspects,
2. Teaching-Learning and Evaluation,
3. Research, Innovations and Extension,
4. Infrastructure and Learning Resources,
5. Student Support and Progression,
6. Governance, Leadership and Management,
7. Institutional Values and Best Practices.

- Accreditation is a process of output quality assurance and improvement, whereby every programme in an approved Institution is critically appraised to verify that the Institution and the programmes continue to meet and/or exceed the ***Norms and Standards*** prescribed by regulator from time to time.

- The purpose of the accreditation by **NBA** is to promote quality education in the accredited **program** and recognize excellence in higher education in colleges and universities, at both the undergraduate and post graduate levels. Through accreditation, the following main purposes are served.
- Support and advice to technical institutions in the maintenance and enhancement of their quality of provision.
- Confidence and assurance on quality to various stakeholders including students.
- Assurance of the good standing of an Institution to government departments and other interested bodies.
- Enabling an Institution to state publicly that it has voluntarily accepted independent inspection and has satisfied all the requirements for satisfactory operation and maintenance of quality in education.

Accreditation is a tool that stakeholders use to monitor, assess and evaluate the standards and quality of the education a student receives at a college, university or other institution of higher learning. Some of the major benefits enrolled students receive by attending an accredited institution / program are as follows:

- Accredited institution / program offers the highest quality education available.
- Accredited institution / program strengthens consumer's confidence, employers value degrees of an accredited program at the higher level.

- Accreditation helps institutions to know their strengths, weaknesses and opportunities, which pushes them to continuously improve their programs and give them a new sense of direction, identity and targets; and
- Accredited institution / program demonstrates accountability to the public, commitment to excellence and continuous quality improvement.

7.7 OPPORTUNITIES:

Quality assurance and graded accreditation systems presents several opportunities:

- **Enhanced Institutional Reputation:** Accreditation and high-quality standards enhance the reputation and credibility of educational institutions.
- **Student Confidence:** Students and parents can make informed decisions about their education based on accreditation status and quality grades.
- **Access to Funding:** Accredited institutions are more likely to receive funding and support from government bodies and other organizations.
- **Global Recognition:** Accreditation and quality assurance align institutions with international standards, facilitating global recognition and collaboration.

7.8 Challenges:

Despite the benefits, there are challenges associated with quality assurance and graded accreditation:

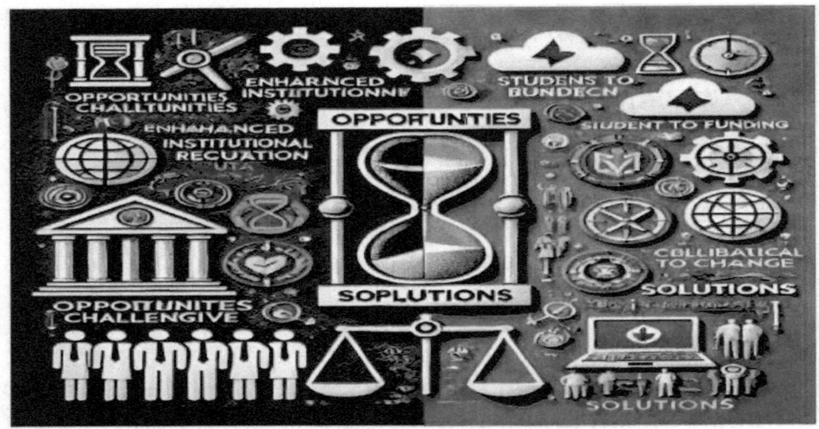

- **Resource Intensive:** The accreditation process can be time-consuming and resource-intensive, requiring significant investment in terms of money, personnel, and effort.
- **Compliance Burden:** Institutions may face challenges in meeting and maintaining compliance with accreditation standards and requirements.
- **Resistance to Change:** There may be resistance from faculty and staff to adopt new practices and changes required for accreditation.
- **Consistency and Fairness:** Ensuring consistency and fairness in the accreditation process across different institutions can be challenging.
- **Parameter Verification**: For verifying the documents/claims/processes submitted by the Institution for accreditation, it is required to develop a system which is independent of Human Intervention and is only system dependent.

- **Acceptance of Accreditation:** The concerned Institution should also accept the Accreditation Grade awarded by the established process, and the transparency of the process should be ensured.

7.9 POSSIBLE SOLUTIONS:

To address these challenges, the following solutions can be considered:

- **Capacity Building:** Providing training and support to institutions to help them prepare for the accreditation process and meet the required standards.
- **Streamlined Processes:** Simplifying and streamlining accreditation procedures to reduce the administrative burden on institutions.
- **Collaborative Approach:** Encouraging collaboration and knowledge-sharing among institutions to foster a culture of continuous improvement and best practices.
- **Technological Integration:** Leveraging technology to facilitate the accreditation process, including data collection, reporting, and communication with accrediting bodies.

By adopting these solutions, NEP-2020 aims to ensure that educational institutions in India deliver high-quality education and continuously improve their standards, thereby enhancing the overall quality of the education system.

CHAPTER-8 SELF-DEVELOPMENT & RESEARCH

Researchers see the "impossible" as the inevitable. The value of getting to your research goals lies NOT in reaching the goal, but what the findings/ openings/ innovations the journey reveals to you.

8.1 RESEARCH

Research is a systematic and organized process of investigating, analysing, and generating knowledge or

information about a particular topic or subject.

- It involves gathering and evaluating data, studying existing literature, formulating hypotheses or research questions, designing methodologies, conducting experiments or studies, analysing the findings, and drawing conclusions.
- The primary goal of research is to contribute to the existing body of knowledge, address gaps in understanding, explore new ideas, or solve problems.
- It can be conducted in various fields such as science, social sciences, humanities, technology, a combination of these and many more.

- Research often follows a structured approach, adhering to specific methodologies and principles, to ensure reliability, validity, testing and replicability of findings.
- The outcomes of research can include new discoveries, advancements in theory or practice, development of innovative technologies, policy recommendations, or improvements in existing knowledge.

8.2 Historical Background

- India has a long historical tradition of research and knowledge creation, in disciplines ranging from science and mathematics to art and literature to phonetics and languages to medicine and agriculture.
- This needs to be further strengthened to make India lead research and innovation in the current century.
- The societal challenges that India needs to address today such as access for all its citizens to clean drinking water and sanitation, quality education and healthcare, improved transportation, air quality, energy, and infrastructure, will require solutions that are rooted in a deep understanding of the social sciences and humanities, and the various socio-cultural and environmental dimensions of the nation.
- A robust ecosystem of research is perhaps more important than ever with the rapid changes occurring in the world today, e.g., in the realm of climate change, population dynamics and management, biotechnology, an expanding digital marketplace, and the rise of machine learning and artificial intelligence.
- Research and innovation at educational

institutions in India, particularly those that are engaged in higher education, is critical at this juncture.

- Evidence from the world's best universities throughout history shows that the good teaching and learning processes at the higher education level occur in environment where there is also a strong culture of research and knowledge creation; conversely, much of the very best research in the world has occurred in multidisciplinary university settings.

Innovation in Research is synonymous with risk-taking and organizations that create revolutionary products or services take on the greatest risk, because they create new markets.

8.3 Need-based research

Need-based research refers to a type of research that aims to identify and understand the needs, desires, and

preferences of a particular target audience or market segment.

It is conducted to gather insights and information about the specific requirements and expectations of individuals or groups in order to develop products, services, or solutions that address those needs effectively.

Here are the key steps involved in conducting need-

based research:

- **Define the research objectives**: Clearly establish and state the purpose and goals of your research. What problem or need are you trying to address?
- **Define the need statement of research:** Define the need statement of research objectives clearly. Recognition of need itself is a creative process. What similar problems exist in other areas whose solution might give some clue? Can denying the problem help in doing away with the problem itself ?
- **Consider product as a source of study**: What is most primitive form of product? How has it developed over the years? Is any idea dropped earlier worth re-introducing. Can you think of so far unused principles to achieve the function? How is product aesthetics? Is there a distinct tendency in a group of users to accepts or reject a specific style/ colour/ form/shape/ application/ function. Identify product environment. Is it domestic, industrial, festive, administrative, and religious? Does it affect design?
- **Identify the target audience**: Determine the specific group or segment of people whose needs you want to study. This could be based on demographic factors (age, gender, education & background, attitude, location) or psychographic factors (interests,

values, lifestyle) or seasonal factors (festivals, seasons, specific occasions), financial strength (spending habits, economic position, social status, motivation to buy the product). Why non-users are not buying the product and how they are managing without it ? Who chooses the product for the user ? Is it the user/ the parents/ the family/ the group ? What significant considerations are given at the time of buying? Can we single out a substantially large group of buyers whose needs are different? Identify the priority given in selecting the particular model of the product (aesthetic reasons, functional reasons, performance, ease in maintenance, tradition). Is any operation taking irritably long time? Is maintenance process irritating ?

- **Gather data:** Employ various research methods to collect relevant data. This can include surveys, interviews, focus groups, observations, or secondary research through existing sources such as market reports, industry studies, or academic publications.
- **Analyse the data**: Once you have collected the data, analyse it to identify patterns, trends, and insights related to the needs and preferences of your target audience. Look for common themes, trouble points, and areas of opportunity.
- **Interpret the findings**: Interpret the research findings in the context of your objectives. What do the results mean for your product, service, or solution? Are there any clear gaps or opportunities that need to be addressed?
- **Develop solutions**: Based on the insights gained from the research, brainstorm and develop potential

solutions that align with the identified needs. This could involve creating new products or services, modifying existing offerings, or improving the customer experience.

- **Test and iterate**: Implement the proposed solutions in a controlled environment and gather feedback from your target audience. Use this feedback to refine and iterate your solutions, ensuring they effectively address the identified needs.
- **Implement and evaluate**: Finally, implement the refined solutions and monitor their performance. Continuously evaluate and measure the impact of your solutions on satisfying the identified needs. Adjust as necessary to optimize the outcomes.

By conducting need-based research, organizations can gain a deep understanding of their target audience's requirements, which helps them develop products and services that are more likely to be successful in the market. This research-driven approach reduces the risk of developing solutions that do not meet customer needs. It increases the likelihood of achieving customer satisfaction and business success.

Here are some key points related to need-based research as per the NEP 2020:

- **Promotion of Research and Innovation**: The NEP 2020 emphasizes the promotion of research and innovation at all levels of education, including school education, higher education, and vocational education. It encourages the development of a research-oriented mindset among students and educators.
- **Focus on Multidisciplinary and**

Interdisciplinary Research: The NEP 2020 highlights the significance of multidisciplinary and interdisciplinary research, encouraging the integration of various disciplines to address complex problems and foster holistic understanding.

- **Strengthening Research Infrastructure**: It emphasizes the need to provide adequate support and funding for research activities, including the establishment of research centres and laboratories.
- **Collaboration and Partnerships**: It emphasizes the importance of collaboration and partnerships between educational institutions, industry, research organizations, and community stakeholders.
- **Research in Teacher Education**: It promotes the inclusion of research components in teacher training programs to enhance the quality of teaching and learning practices and orient thought process of teachers towards research.
- **Research for Social and Economic Development**: It encourages research that addresses societal challenges, supports sustainable development goals, and promotes inclusive growth.

8.4 National Research Foundation (NRF)

- The National Research Foundation (NRF) is an organization that exists in various countries around the world to support and promote research and development activities within the country.
- The specific roles and specific objectives of the NRF is to foster a strong research culture, advance scientific knowledge, and drive innovation.
- It plays a crucial role in providing financial support, grants, scholarships, and fellowships to researchers,

scientists, and students.

- The NRF may also establish research centres, laboratories, and provide support to facilitate cutting-edge research and promote collaboration among researchers.
- In addition to funding research projects, the NRF may be responsible for setting research priorities, developing research policies, evaluating research outcomes, establishing national research strategies, promoting interdisciplinary research, and supporting initiatives that address societal challenges.
- '**Anusandhan**' National Research Foundation (ANRF) has been established in India to accelerate the research activities in the Universities. The first meeting was held on 10th September 2024 chaired by Prime Minister, showing the seriousness of the Government in implementation of NEP.

National Research Foundation (NRF) Activities are:

- It will be governed, *independently* of the government, by a **rotating Board of Governors** consisting of the very best researchers and innovators across fields.
- Enable a culture of research to permeate through our universities.
- Provide a reliable base of merit-based but equitable peer-reviewed research funding.
- Fund competitive, peer-reviewed grant proposals of all types and across all disciplines
- Provide research facilitate at academic institutions, particularly at universities and colleges where ***research is currently in a nascent stage***, and

through mentoring of such institutions.

• Act as a ***liaison*** between researchers and government as well as industry, so that research scholars are constantly made aware of the most urgent national research issues, and policymakers are constantly made aware of the latest research breakthroughs.

8.5 National Research Foundation (NRF) for Researchers

There are some general aspects of NRF that are often beneficial for researchers:

• **Research Funding**: One of the primary roles of an NRF is to provide financial support for research projects. They offer competitive grants and funding programs that researchers can apply for to secure resources for their research activities, including equipment, materials, travel, and personnel.

Fellowships and Scholarships: These programs offer financial support for individuals pursuing research

degrees (such as Ph.D. or postdoctoral fellowships) or conducting independent research projects.

- **Research Infrastructure and Facilities**: NRFs invest in developing research infrastructure and facilities to enhance the research capabilities within a country, that can include establishing research centres, laboratories, and shared resources that researchers can access to conduct their research more effectively.
- **Collaboration and Networking Opportunities**: NRFs facilitate support for international collaborations and partnerships, promoting knowledge exchange and enhancing research outcomes.
- **Research Excellence and Recognition**: NRFs administer programs that recognize and reward research excellence, and include prestigious awards, grants for outstanding researchers, or initiatives to promote innovative and impactful research projects.
- **Research Policy Development:** NRF works closely with government agencies and policymakers

to identify research priorities, develop funding frameworks, and advocate for research-related issues.
- **Research Capacity Building**: NRFs support research capacity building by providing training

programs, mentorship opportunities, and professional development resources for researchers.

- **Data and Knowledge Management**: NRFs may have initiatives that include data sharing policies, open access initiatives, or platforms for disseminating research findings to the broader community.

8.6 National Research Foundation (NRF) for students

Here are some ways in which an NRF will benefit students:

- **Research Scholarships and Fellowships**: NRFs

administer scholarship and fellowship programs that support research students or conducting research projects, and offer financial support to cover tuition fees, living expenses, and research-related costs.

- **Undergraduate Research Programs**: These programs can provide funding, mentorship, and resources for students to conduct research projects, gain hands-on experience, and develop research skills foe UG Research.

- **Research Internships and Exchanges**: These opportunities expose students to cutting-edge research, enhance their knowledge, and expand their professional networks.

- **Research Grants for Students**: These grants can support student-led research projects, covering expenses such as research materials, travel, and dissemination of findings.
- **Research Conferences and Competitions**: These events provide platforms for students to present their findings, receive feedback, and connect with peers and experts in their field.
- **Research Training and Workshops**: These initiatives provide guidance on research methodologies, ethics, data analysis, and academic writing, equipping students with the necessary tools for conducting research.
- **Research Networking and Collaboration**: These interactions can lead to partnerships with other students, researchers, and industry professionals, fostering interdisciplinary collaborations and expanding student's research horizons.
- **Research Publications and Dissemination Support**: This helps students gain recognition for their research contributions and disseminate their findings to a wider audience.

8.7 INCLUSION OF RESEARCH AND INTERNSHIPS IN THE UNDERGRADUATE CURRICULUM

The inclusion of research and internships in the UG curriculum offers significant benefits to students by

providing them with practical experiences, real-world skills, and opportunities for personal and professional growth. Here are some reasons why the inclusion is valuable in the UG curriculum:

- **Hands-on Learning**: Research and internships provide students with hands-on learning experiences that go beyond theoretical knowledge. They allow students to apply classroom concepts and theories to real-world problems, enhancing their understanding and competence in their field of study.
- **Skill Development**: Engaging in research and internships helps students develop a wide range of skills, including critical thinking, problem-solving, communication, teamwork, and project management.
- **Career Exploration**: Research and internships provide opportunities for students to explore different career paths and industries, gain exposure to professional environments, build networks, and make

informed decisions about their future career goals.

- **Mentorship and Guidance**: Research and internship experiences often involve working closely with mentors or supervisors who provide guidance and support.
- **Building a Professional Network**: Through research and internships, students have the chance to connect with professionals in their field of interest, for future employment opportunities, internships, or collaborations.
- **Personal and Professional Growth**: Engaging in research and internships promotes personal and professional growth by challenging students to step out of their comfort zones, take initiative, and develop a strong work ethic.
- **Contribution to Knowledge and Society**: It allows students to explore new ideas, address important questions, and make meaningful contributions to their field of study.

It is important for universities and colleges to provide adequate resources, support, and mentorship to ensure a meaningful and inclusive experience for all students, regardless of their background or prior experience.

8.8 Internationalization at home

It aims to provide students with global perspectives, cross-cultural understanding, and opportunities for engagement with diverse cultures, without the need for physical mobility or study abroad experiences. This concept recognizes that not all students have the means or opportunity to participate in traditional study abroad programs. Therefore, it focuses on creating an inclusive and diverse learning environment that prepares students to thrive in an interconnected world. Here are some key elements and strategies commonly associated with internationalization at home:

- **Intercultural Competence**: This involves

providing students with opportunities to engage with diverse cultures, challenge their assumptions, and develop skills to navigate and communicate across cultural boundaries.

- **Curricular Integration**: This can be achieved by infusing international topics, case studies, and comparative analyses into existing courses or developing new courses that explore global issues.

- **International and Multicultural Events**: These events may include international festivals, guest lectures, workshops, film screenings, and cultural performances.
- **Language Learning:** It provides an opportunity for students to engage with different languages and cultures, even if they are not studying abroad.
- **Collaboration and Partnerships**: These collaborations can enrich the learning experience and foster connections across borders for collaborative research, joint projects, virtual exchange programs, and intercultural dialogues.
- **Faculty and Staff Development**: Training programs, workshops, and conferences can enhance educator's intercultural competence and teaching methodologies.
- **Campus Support Services**: Offering support services can facilitate the integration and well-being of international students and foster interactions between domestic and international students.

8.9 INTERNATIONALIZATION IN THE HIGHER EDUCATION

It involves promoting global awareness, cross-cultural understanding, and collaboration among students, faculty, and institutions worldwide.

The key objectives of internationalization in higher education are:

- **Global Perspective**: Providing students with a broader understanding of global issues, cultures, and perspectives, and preparing them to be active global citizens.
- **Academic Excellence**: Enhancing the quality of education through the exchange of knowledge, ideas,

and best practices with international partners, and fostering international research collaborations.

- **Student Mobility**: Encouraging student mobility through study abroad programs, student exchanges,

and internships, which enable students to gain international experience and develop intercultural competencies.

- **Curriculum Internationalization**: Infusing international and cross-cultural content into the curriculum to expose students to diverse perspectives and global challenges, ensuring graduates are equipped with global competence.
- **Research Collaboration**: Promoting international research collaborations, joint projects, and partnerships with universities and research institutions around the world, leading to knowledge creation and innovation.
- **Institutional Partnerships**: Establishing strategic partnerships and networks with international institutions to foster collaboration in areas such as

student and faculty exchange, joint degree programs, and research initiatives.

- **Recruitment and Diversity**: Attracting a diverse student body and faculty from different countries, fostering an inclusive environment, and promoting cultural exchange within the campus community.
- **International Student Support**: Providing comprehensive support services to international students, including academic advising, language support, and assistance with cultural adaptation and integration.
- **Global Engagement**: Engaging in international development projects, community outreach, and service-learning initiatives that address global challenges and contribute to the sustainable development of communities worldwide.

8.10 Self Improvement & Development:

Self-improvement and development are crucial for both educators and students in achieving personal and professional growth. The focus is on fostering a culture of continuous learning and self-reflection to

enhance skills, knowledge, and overall well-being.

- **Lifelong Learning:** Encouraging a mindset of lifelong learning to keep pace with advancements in knowledge and technology.
- **Professional Development:** Participating in workshops, seminars, and training programs to acquire new skills and stay updated with industry trends.
- **Personal Growth:** Engaging in activities that promote personal well-being, such as mindfulness, fitness, and hobbies.
- **Reflective Practice:** Regularly reflecting on one's own practices, identifying areas for improvement, and setting goals for personal and professional development.

8.11 Research, Patents, Books, and other Academic Materials:

Research and the creation of academic materials are fundamental to advancing knowledge and contributing to societal development.

- **Research Initiatives:** Encouraging faculty and students to engage in cutting-edge research projects that address real-world problems.
- **Funding and Grants:** Securing funding and grants from various sources to support research activities and innovation.
- **Publication and Dissemination:** Promoting the publication of research findings in reputable journals, books, and conferences to disseminate knowledge widely.

- **Intellectual Property:** Supporting the patenting process to protect and commercialize innovative ideas

and inventions.

- **Collaborative Research:** Fostering collaborations with other institutions, industry, and international partners to enhance research quality and impact.

8.12 Opportunities:

The emphasis on self-development and research presents numerous opportunities:

- **Enhanced Skill Sets:** Continuous self-improvement leads to the development of new skills and competencies, making individuals more adaptable and employable.
- **Innovation and Creativity:** A focus on research and development fosters innovation and creativity, leading to new discoveries and advancements.
- **Institutional Reputation:** High-quality research and academic contributions enhance the reputation and credibility of educational institutions.
- **Global Collaboration:** Opportunities for collaboration with international partners expand the

reach and impact of research efforts.

8.13 CHALLENGES:

There are several challenges associated with self-development and research:

- **Resource Constraints:** Limited access to funding, facilities, and resources can hinder research activities and personal development initiatives.
- **Time Management:** Balancing teaching, administrative duties, and research can be challenging for educators and researchers.
- **Quality Assurance:** Ensuring the quality and relevance of research and academic materials can be difficult, especially in rapidly evolving fields.
- **Intellectual Property Issues:** Navigating the complexities of patenting and protecting intellectual property requires expertise and support.
- **Fabrication or falsification of data as per the hypothesis:** Falsification of fabricated data to suit the hypothesis is a big issue and constitutes about 5% of the misconduct.
- **Plagiarism:** All types of plagiarism constitutes about 25% of misconduct and must be arrested to ascertain the quality of research.
- Problematic data presentation or analysis.
- Failure to obtain ethical approval.
- Inappropriate claims of authorship.
- Duplicate publication.
- Undisclosed conflict of interest (COI).
- Duplicate submission/ redundant publication.
- GIFTED misconduct.
- GHOST authors.
- Conflict of Interest.

- Fraud.
- Unreasonable copying.
- Duplicate publication.
- Bad Citation.

8.14 Possible Solutions:

To address these challenges, the following solutions can be considered:

- **Supportive Policies:** Implementing policies that provide time, resources, and incentives for self-development and research activities.
- **Funding Opportunities:** Increasing access to funding through grants, scholarships, and partnerships with industry and government.
- **Mentorship Programs:** Establishing mentorship programs to guide and support individuals in their self-development and research activities.
- **Collaborative Platforms:** Creating platforms for collaboration and knowledge-sharing among researchers, institutions, and industry partners.
- **Streamlined Processes:** Simplifying administrative processes related to research, publication, and patenting to reduce bureaucratic hurdles and enhance efficiency.
- **Each one Teach one:** The researchers may own a fellow researcher in the same area of study, and decide to clarify all his doubts/queries.
- Group Learning for conceptual topics
- Attending mutually delivered Seminars
- Group Learning on use of ICT facility
- **Group Learning by denying a fact**: In Group learning activity, the audience may deny a fact presented by the speaker, and thus force the speaker to

offer an alternate explanation, and in the process may discover some new concept.

- **Ongoing In-house Research Activities OIRA:** Workshops on Ongoing *In-house* Research Activities in the University may be conducted to share Research being conducted.
- Club Innovation on Research
- Self-assessment of ongoing research among Scholars.

By leveraging these opportunities and addressing the challenges, NEP-2020 aims to foster a culture of self-improvement, innovation, and research excellence in educational institutions, contributing to the overall development of individuals and society.

www.ingramcontent.com/pod-product-compliance
Lightning Source LLC
LaVergne TN
LVHW091318150826
845673LV00006B/1688

* 9 7 9 8 8 9 5 8 8 2 2 3 8 *